GULLY PUBLICATIONS PRESENTS

BANANA PUDDING

A NOVEL BY
Alah Adams

To Charles
Thank you Brother

[signature]

ISBN: 0-9778302-0-9

Graphic Design: Jesus 'Dr. Zuess' Baca for ZUESS DESIGNS
Cover Model: Princess Pursia
Photographer: Duy Tran
Chief Editor: George Clarke
Assistant Editor: Sunita Sabitree Bechan
Co-Editor: Alah Adams

GULLY MULTI-MEDIA, LLC
P.O. Box 3602
Laurel, MD 20707
www.gullymultimedia.com

SPECIAL THANKS...

I want to thank the EVER PRESENT SELF that exists within every living thing. I want to thank my parents Carl D. Adams and Brenda Adams for guiding me into the right direction. I want to give a shout out to all my beautiful kids, Alah Jr., Dejour, Elijah, and my baby girl, Audrey. Daddy loves you. A very special thanks to my children's mother's for blessing me with such beautiful kids. Thanks to my siblings Carl Jr., Carl Vic, Kiesha, and Maquan for your support. A special thanks goes out to Amos Pierre, my brother from another mother and business partner. Katina, I appreciate all your efforts. Tanecia, thanks for believing in my work so strongly that we broke down barriers! Johnny Nunez for always helping out the little guys! Lots of people have come and gone, but the people that matter remain on the team. I want to thank my Aunt Yvonne for believing in me and my whole family for encouraging me to keep writing. A special thank you to Lynn Pacillio, you told me to keep writing, and I did! Another special thank you to my high school sweetheart Sab for believing in me enough to make things happen.

       To my comrade, Big Brook you always encouraged me to keep it going. To all my comrades behind the wall, hold your head up. Change the game when you get out. This book was written as a testament to anyone that has ever gone through hell only to come out right. Remember that life is precious, so live every day to the fullest. I hope that you enjoy reading my work; I put my most positive energy into every word. I will leave you with these words of wisdom: LIMITED KNOWLEDGE IS BONDAGE!

CHAPTER 1

Trina entered the lavish condo and walked into the lavender colored bedroom. Her best friend, Monica, was out cold from another wild night of partying.

"Girl, get your ass up!" Trina yelled, interrupting Monica's slumber. "It's 12 o'clock in the afternoon. Are you some type of vampire? Sleep all day party all night."

"Leave me alone! Can't you see that I'm tired?" Monica said with a throat full of gravel. "I was at the club until 6 this morning, and then I went to take care of some business."

"I guess you forgot about Tavon's birthday party today." Tavon was Trina's 4 year old son.

"Oh shit, girl. I'm sorry." Monica halfway came to life. "Just give me one more hour of rest. I'll be there... I promise."

Trina looked at her with a cynical half smile before walking out of the condo. Trina and Monica have been friends since the third grade. Both of them had grown up to be beautiful women. Trina was the shorter of the two. She had a smooth mocha-colored complexion with very nicely shaped eyes and full lips. Trina had developed child bearing hips, which gave her butt a nice shape.

Monica was light skinned with green eyes and the body of a goddess. She had a backside that would put J-LO to shame. She had perfect 36c size breasts that stood at attention like a soldier giving a salute. Though Trina was just as beautiful, Monica seemed to attract more attention. It was no secret that Monica was a man magnet.

Both women had their share of bad relationships with men. Trina had just broken up with her son's father, Rome, after a seven-year relationship. After catching Rome cheating several times, she called it quits; Trina couldn't take it anymore. They remained friends and still had sex from time to time.

Rome was a good father to their son, Tavon. He was there for his son from day one. Tavon loved his father; Rome was his hero. Despite Rome's incessant womanizing, he was a good dude.

Trina and Monica were both 25 years old and both were Taurus's, one of the reasons they were so close. Trina was a week older than Monica, so she played the role of big sister. Trina would always say, "Remember, I'm older than you," whenever she wanted to get a point across.

Monica learned about men early in her life. She was in love one time when she was 18. She got hurt that one time and vowed never to get played again. Since then, she has been the one doing the playing.

She would always tell Trina that she was stupid for letting Rome play her. Monica would say, "He's a dog like the rest of them." Trina finally took her advice and left Rome. Even though they were still having sex, they weren't together as a couple.

Monica is a player in every sense of the word. Most would consider her a Ho or a Slut bucket, even a prostitute. Let Monica tell it, she was taking advantage of her assets; her looks and her body.

Everything she owned was paid for by sympathetic men who just wanted to be in her presence. Most of them would not get any sex with her unless they were willing to pay the price. For a mere fifteen hundred, a man could taste her pudding; just a little bit.

That little bit would open their noses enough to keep them spending more money. Some of the men went bankrupt and when the money was gone, so was she. Her motto was, 'You have to pay to play'. She stuck to it like the law.

Monica was living the life of a Queen. She owned a brand new BMW 645. Her condo was decked with marble tiles and plush Persian rugs. Her furniture was made from calf suede. She had plasma screens throughout the house.

Her wardrobe read like a who's who of the fashion industry. Dolce & Gabana, Chloe and H. Vendel, you name it, she had it. And when something new came out, she was the first to own it.

Monica wore a tennis bracelet with five carats of VVS diamonds, a pair of two-carat diamond studs, a ten-carat diamond chain, a lady Rolex with a three-carat bezel, and a three-carat diamond ring. Together, she wore a total of twenty-five carats. All her bling was paid for by weak-minded men who would fall victim to her game.

She praised herself as being one of the best who has ever done it. She was very overzealous and cocky. Coming from Bedford-Stuyvesant Brooklyn with nothing --to grinding her way to having luxury-- was a major accomplishment for her.

Monica grew up very poor, in a dysfunctional family. Both of her parents were heroin addicts. She could never forget the many nights she went to bed hungry. Those memories motivated her to get more from life.

Those hard times fueled the fire for her relentless approach to life.

Both of Monica's parents died from HIV due to intravenous drug use. She had no siblings, and the few family members she had, were in Columbia, South Carolina. The only family she had in New York was Trina and Trina's family. They took her in after her parents passed.

Although Monica got lots of money from men, she does have a job. It's not a regular 9 to 5, like a nurse or a secretary. Monica is a professional dancer, a fancy word for stripper. That's where she met all of her tricks. She stripped at Sue's Rendezvous, a very upscale gentleman's club in Mount Vernon. She started working there on her 18th birthday. The rest is history.

Monica is the club's main attraction. Men come from miles around just too see her show. Without her presence there, Sue's was just like all the other strip clubs.

Monica learned at a young age that she had attractive power over men. When she was 13, a flashy drug dealer named Big Ed was her first victim. Big Ed sold drugs to her parents. Every time he came to her apartment, he would try hard to get at Monica. Monica hated him. She thought he was ugly. Nevertheless, Big Ed never gave up.

"Hey sexy, you want to ride in my BM?" Ed would ask desperately.

"No, I don't." Monica would answer with an attitude.

"One day I'm going to have you. I always get what I want."

It went on like this until the summer before Monica's freshman year in high school. All the kids from Monica's neighborhood were going school shopping; all, except Monica. In Brooklyn, it didn't matter if you were pretty. If you were a bum, people dissed you, and young Monica wore two-year old hand me downs.

Monica sat on the stoop of her building, feeling depressed. That's when Tookie, the older girl from upstairs, came down and sat with her. Tookie knew Monica's situation and that her parents did not provide for her. Tookie also knew that if Monica had gear, she would be the prettiest chick in the hood.

"What's up Monica? Why you look so down?" asked Tookie.

"No reason. It's just that I want to go school shopping like everyone else."

"I'm going to tell you something. Nobody's going to do anything for you in this world. If you don't do it for yourself, it won't get done." Tookie paused to look in Monica's eyes. "Listen, I see the way Big Ed be sweating you. If you give him some coochie, he will buy you all the school clothes you need."

"I hate him. He is so ugly."

"He might be ugly, but he got money. You'll learn when you get older. Men with money will pay to play, unlike these broke ass niggas out here."

Monica soaked in what Tookie was saying. Although she hated Big Ed, she loved to dress nicely. She thought about it and decided it wouldn't be a bad idea. At least I can be fly for my freshman year, she thought.

The next day when she saw Big Ed, Monica had her plan all mapped out. As usual, he approached her and said something. "What's up sexy? I'm still waiting for you."

To his surprise, Monica gave him the most radiant smile. "You are? I've been thinking, if I was your girl I know you would take care of me," Monica responded.

"Of course, so what are you saying? You want to be my girl?"

"Sure. But how would I know if you're not playing me?"

"I would never play you. I've been trying to get with you forever. How can I prove myself?"

"You really want to know?" She paused and gave him a sexy look with her green eyes. "Take me shopping for school."

"That's all? Come on, let's go shopping."

They went downtown Brooklyn to Al B Square Mall and Big Ed splurged a thousand dollars on Monica. She's never had so many clothes before. She had all the latest wear. He even bought her an x&o chain and earrings.

"Damn, it was that easy...I didn't even have to give him any sex," she said to herself. Her natural women's intuition kicked in. "If it was that easy, maybe I can stall on giving him sex for a while. I'll just be real nice to him. That should satisfy him for now."

She was right. She would be very polite to him and kiss him on the cheek. He kept spending money on her. He liked to be seen driving around with a pretty girl in his BMW.

Before Big Ed got a chance to have sex with Monica, he was gunned down over a drug beef. Monica was saddened by his demise. He treated her like a Queen.

No one in her young life had showed her that much love and concern.

That was her first lesson in her magical powers over men. Since then, she has developed her powers to its peak. She felt that no man alive could resist her powers of seduction. Every player meets her match. For now, she was like Mike Tyson in his prime...UNDISPUTED.

CHAPTER 2

Tavon's birthday party was held at the Discovery Zone. It was a nice place to have a birthday party for a 4 year old. There were lots of fun things for all the kids to do. There were kids everywhere, running around laughing and playing.

All of Tavon's friends from the neighborhood were there. His father, Rome, even invited his manager, Adonis, and his daughter, Makeda. Rome was an aspiring Rap artist. He had been trying to land a record deal since he was 16. Now at 28, his hip hop biological clock was running out. Rap fans don't gravitate towards old rappers. The average rapper's career is over at 35. Unlike other genres, rap caters generally to the young and the restless.

For the first time in his career, it looked like he would get signed to a record deal. Under the professional guide of Adonis, Rome was seeing a glimpse of the lime light.

Adonis owned and operated his own artist management firm called Star Quality. He had a stable of 5 successful artists. Four of them were R&B artists; Rome was the only rap artist. With rap becoming such a huge commodity, Adonis felt that he should add more rappers to his roster.

He already had three record labels that were considering signing Rome. With a track record like Adonis's, it would be no time before Rome achieved his goal.

Adonis was what women called a rare Black Man. Women found him extremely attractive. Once they held a conversation with him, they were astonished by his intellect. His favorite subject was African History. He prided himself for knowing his history.

Adonis especially liked Egyptian history. He considered himself a self-proclaimed Egyptologist. He even thought of himself as a direct decedent of the Egyptians. Considering that the original Egyptians were Black, every Black Man resembled them.

At 6'4, with a very muscular frame, Adonis stood out. His skin was a smooth peanut butter brown complexion. He had innocent hazel eyes and curly hair. His smile could brighten up a room. Most women couldn't help but notice him. However, he was very humble, not at all pompous about his looks. Since he was a teen, he had a flock of girls wanting to be his.

Adonis was a single father. His wife, Tammy, was killed in a car accident a year ago. Between working hard for himself and raising his daughter, he didn't have time for dating. When he did feel lonely, he would reminisce about Tammy. He missed her a lot. No woman could ever take her place.

"Thanks for inviting us to Tavon's party. Makeda needed to get out and mingle with other kids. She doesn't get out much," said Adonis.

"Hey, that's what friends are for." Rome held out his hand for a handshake. "Remember the chick I told you about?"

"Yeah, but I'm not trying to meet anyone right now. It's only been a year since Tammy's death and..."

Just then, as if her timing was destined, Monica entered the Discovery Zone. She looked like an R&B diva. Rome didn't have to say anything; the look on Adonis' face said it all. Adonis was in a trance staring across the room at Monica.

Adonis tried to keep his composure by being cool and calm. He showed no sign of over attraction to Monica; that wasn't his style. Although, in his mind he was like, DAMN!

Monica made her way through the sea of playful children to the area where her friend, Trina, was sitting.

"Hey girl, I told you I'd make it."

"You better had made it because Tavon would never forgive you."

"I wouldn't have missed it for the world." As Monica spoke those last words, she looked across the room with a blank expression on her face. It was like she couldn't fathom what she was seeing. It was Adonis she was looking at. She had a dreamy look in her eyes, as if she was hypnotized.

Trina looked at her friend with confusion on her face. She turned her head to see what it was that had Monica in such a trance. Then she realized what Monica was looking at.

"Damn girl, wake up!" Trina said in a loud tone. "You were just in the Twilight Zone."

Monica snapped out of her fixation like a patient coming out of hypnosis. "Trina, who is that guy standing over there with Rome?"

"Oh, that's Rome's new manager. His name is Adonis."

"Adonis...He is a don."

"Yes, he is," Trina said, confirming her friend's adoration. "Girl, he is fine as hell."

Rome and Adonis were making their way over to where Trina and Monica were standing. The closer Adonis came to Monica, the more she felt her vagina flutter. She was starting to feel moisture in her panties. She had never felt like this way about a man before. By the time Adonis was in arms reach of Monica, she had the sudden urge to urinate.

"Monica, this is Adonis," Rome said as Adonis stuck out his hand.

"It's nice to meet you, Monica." Adonis gripped her hand and kissed it.

Monica's whole body did a slight shake. Something was happening and she couldn't explain it. She felt speechless. She slowly blinked her eyes and abruptly said, "Excuse me." Monica dashed to the restroom to try to compose herself.

Adonis, Rome, and Trina all looked at each other bemused at Monica's sudden departure. Trina shrugged her shoulders and raised her eyebrows in a gesture of confusion. She had never seen her friend react this way.

Monica was in the bathroom stall sitting on the toilet. "What the fuck just happened?" she asked herself out loud.

Trina went to the bathroom to see what was wrong with Monica. She saw Monica's feet under the stall. "Monica, are you all right?"

"I'm OK. I just drank too much last night. I felt like I was going to throw up."

Monica was too embarrassed to tell Trina what really happened. She didn't even know how to explain what just happened even if she did want to tell Trina.

"You sure you're OK?"

"I'm OK. I'll be out in a minute." Monica sat on the toilet getting her thoughts together. This guy must be really special, she thought to herself. She had met many handsome men and none of them affected her like this. Maybe he is the one, she thought. No, fuck that, she thought, dismissing the notion that Adonis could be the one.

She came out of the stall and looked herself over in the mirror. Everything was perfect. She arched her back a little to give her breast that extra perky look. Then she turned to the side to see her butt; it was round as ever. She walked out to face Adonis one more time.

As Monica reached the threesome, they were all focusing their attention on her.

"Are you alright, Monica?" Adonis asked with genuine concern.

"Yes, I'm OK. My stomach was feeling a little queasy."

"Well, Monica, what do you do for a living?" inquired Adonis.

"I'm a model for Fresh Faces." That was Monica's alibi for her real occupation. Trina was the only one who knew what Monica really did.

"Oh, Fresh Faces. I have an artist who models for them. Are you familiar with the R&B singer, Grace?"

"Of course, her music is banging. But I don't know her from the agency."

"When she isn't recording or touring, she is modeling. She is the busiest artist that I manage."

Adonis couldn't help but notice all the diamonds that Monica was wearing. Her ears, neck, and fingers were blinging off of the lights. She must get a lot of work at Fresh Faces, Adonis thought to himself.

"Which designers have you modeled for?"

"I do mostly Victoria Secrets, but I've done Armani and Versace also." Monica answered like an expert liar.

"I'll be sure to keep an eye out for you next time I'm browsing through her catalogue."

Their conversation was interrupted by the ringing of Monica's cell phone. This line was for business only. She pulled the phone out from her Coach bag.

"Excuse me, Adonis." Monica said.

It was one of her tricks. He was a wealthy banker named Timothy Stewart. Whenever he had free time, he would call Monica for her services. He didn't want sex though. He was into S&M. Timothy liked to be tied up and spanked, or walked around like a dog with a leash on. Monica didn't enjoy spanking Timothy, but for $1500 an hour, she dealt with it. His favorite game was called the Plantation Game. Monica played the role of the slave master and Timothy played the slave.

"Hello Timmy. I'm not available for the photo shoot right at this moment. I'm at my nephew's birthday party." Monica pretended that he was a photographer.

"When can you come, I need you." Timmy sounded like a crack head. "I'm at our regular meeting spot at the Waldorf." He spoke as if it was a life or death situation.

"I'll be there in an hour and a half."

"OK, it's 3:30, so you'll be here at 5?"

"I'll be there at 5." She hung up. "A models job is never done."

"I see. Maybe we can get together for lunch or dinner some time," suggested Adonis.

13

"Definitely! Matter of fact, I'll give you my numbers." Monica reached into her bag for a pen and a piece of paper. She wrote down her home and cell phone numbers. She usually only gave out her cell number, but Monica felt like any man who can make her feel the way Adonis did, was worth every number she has.

As Monica handed Adonis her numbers, the cutest little girl ran up to him and grabbed his leg. "Daddy, who is she?" Makeda asked with defiance.

"This is Monica." Adonis spoke with uneasiness in his tone. He hadn't had a woman around his daughter since her mother died. "Monica, this is my five year old daughter, Makeda."

"Hi, Makeda. You're so pretty." Makeda just looked at her with a frown on her face.

Makeda was over-protective of her father. Because she was so young when her mother died, Makeda didn't like her father talking to other women. Her father was all that she had.

Monica quickly picked up on the child's vibe. "I'm going to go over there with the birthday boy for a few minutes before I leave." She took a few steps and turned around. Just as she planned, Adonis was staring at her voluptuous butt. "Oh, and use those numbers."

"I most definitely will," said Adonis.

Monica spent the next thirty minutes with Tavon and Trina. They sang Happy Birthday and played games. Monica gave Tavon the present she bought for him. It was a nice gold chain with his name in diamonds. She also bought him two games for his Play Station.

After she gave Tavon his gifts, Monica had to go; Timothy would be waiting for her. Duty calls, she thought, and then she departed.

CHAPTER 3

On her way to the Waldorf Hotel, Monica stopped at her condo to get her whip and cuffs. She was in deep thought. She was thinking about her life and where it was going. The fact that she had to lie to Adonis about her occupation made her feel phony. "Am I ashamed of what I am," she asked herself. This was the first time that her conscience bothered her about lying to a man.

The reality is that anyone who lives a normal lifestyle looks at strippers as low life women. In many ways, some of them can be. Sometimes Monica felt like a piece of meat on display for perverted men to gawk at. This wasn't the first time she had these types of thoughts about her job. This was only the first time that it really bothered her. She usually dismissed the thought and kept it moving. It was something about Adonis that made her begin to look at things differently. She didn't know what it was about him, but she was determined to find out.

When she reached the Waldorf, she became more agitated about what she was about to do. In a way, her having to play out this sick fantasy made her just as sick as him. These men had some real mental issues. It was not normal to want a woman to beat on you. It was equally as abnormal for the woman who participated.

She got to the room five minutes late. Timothy was ready for his beating. He was already stripped down to his boxer shorts and a wife beater tee-shirt. When Monica entered the room, he was happy like a dog at the sight of his owner. She looked at the pale little White Man with pure disgust. The stupid sneer he wore on his thin lips

16

made her want to smack him, so she did. "POW" right on his left facial cheek.

"What the fuck are you smiling for?" she asked like a drill sergeant. "Did I say for you to smile?"

"No. I'm sorry." Timothy responded like an obedient servant.

"Sorry, what?"

"I'm sorry, Massa."

"That's more like it."

She looked around the room. As always, he had the money on the night stand. There was something else on the night stand that was camouflaged so well no one would figure out what it was except Timothy. Timothy had brought a state of the art spy cam that looked like an alarm clock. He only wanted an hour of abuse at a time, but this time he wanted to tape it so he could watch it at home.

"OK, assume the position, you filthy cracker slave. I'll teach you to disobey Massa."

Timothy went to the far wall and put his hands up high on the wall. She took out the whip and cracked it softly on his back the first time. A feeling of disgust came over her. She thought about Adonis and what he would think of her if he knew what she was doing. Monica was sure a nice guy like Adonis wouldn't approve of this. Then Timothy interrupted her thoughts.

"What's wrong, Massa? You're not going to whip me? I've been a bad slave."

She snapped out of her daydream and cracked the whip on his back so hard that he screamed out with agony. She was sure someone else heard him. Then she did it again. This time, Timothy protested. "Ouch! Not so hard. That really hurt."

"Shut the fuck up, you bitch!" Monica said with anger. "Did I tell you to talk?" She hit him again. "Did I?" She cracked him two more times. "You will learn some manners on my plantation." Then she hit him twice. Now she was in a blind rage.

When she finally stopped, she looked at his back. It was bleeding and he had fat welts all over his back. Timothy was silently crying because he didn't want her to get more violent.

Monica shook her head and asked herself, "What the fuck is wrong with me?" She sat down on the bed and dropped the whip. "Sit down Timothy."

"On the floor, Massa?"

"No, on the chair." She spoke in a nice tone. He sat down with tears streaming down his face. "Timothy, you need help. I think you should see a Psych instead of seeing me."

"You really think so Massa?"

"Knock it off with the Massa shit. I'm serious, Timothy. Get yourself some mental help."

She got up and left the room. Her conscience was bothering her so much that she left the money. Maybe I need some help too, she thought as she exited the hotel.

When Monica walked out of the room, Timothy took the memory card out of the clock and inserted it into his phone. He played back some of the footage.

"Assume the position, you filthy cracker!" Monica yelled. The visuals alone almost brought Timothy to a climax.

From the start of Timothy and Monica's foray into S&M, Monica made it clear that she would not allow their sessions to be taped. Timothy offered her three times more money if she would let him tape their sessions. Now he had a least a quarter of a session on tape. "It doesn't matter now Ms. Banana Pudding because now I have a clip of us to satisfy me." Timothy smiled as he watched her in action.

Timothy picked up the money and smiled again, "And I have my money. Today is a good day."

A couple of days had passed and Adonis was too busy to even think about calling Monica. He had gotten confirmation from Artist Records about signing Rome to a deal. At this point in the game, Adonis had to be ready for negotiations between lawyers.

Then there was an issue with another artist. It seems that the label didn't want to push her new album the way they should. That would result in low record sales. The label's beef was that they felt she was established and didn't need big promotions.

Meanwhile, Rome was getting impatient. Even though the deal of his life was finally coming through, he had to eat. It would be at least 6 months before Rome would get a cash advance. Rome was ready to revert back to the only thing he knew how to do besides rap: hustle selling drugs.

If he sold drugs, he knew he would be risking his career and his freedom. With a four year old son and needs of his own, he had to do something.

Adonis knew Rome's situation, but the only thing he could offer him was advice. Adonis learned the hard way about giving artists money. If something went wrong, then he lost out. He tried to get Rome a job, but Rome smoked too much weed and couldn't show up on time.

Rome had lots of issues. He lost his father at the tender age of twelve, and his mother died eight months ago. He started smoking and drinking heavily for a while after his mother's death.

Like so many other young Black males his age, Rome considered himself a thug. The streets were all he really knew. The music industry and drug dealing are the only trades he had under his belt.

Rome and his father were very close. His father was a hardworking man, the breadwinner of the family. He would bring young Rome with him to work. He was a Superintendent of a few buildings in Brooklyn. He would teach young Rome the trade of being a Super.

"Look, son, if you want to go anywhere in life, you have to work hard. You don't get anywhere in life by taking the easy route."

When Rome would think about those words, he wished his father was still alive. Maybe things would be different for me, he thought to himself.

After Rome's father died, he became a troubled youth. He spent time in Juvenile detention. Then, when he was old enough, he did a short stint upstate New York with the big boys. That slowed him down a little. He was still dabbling in the drug game, but nothing serious.

Rome met Adonis six months ago at an open mic show. Adonis approached Rome with his business card after he saw Rome perform. The rest is history.

Rome stopped selling drugs and dedicated his time to perfecting his craft. Under the tutelage of Adonis, his skills as an artist developed. Six months later, and a pocket full of lint, Rome had to make a move.

"Fuck it, son. I'm about to get my hustle on," Rome said to his best friend, PT, through a thick cloud of weed smoke.

"I hear you, son. You know I'm going to hold you down."

"Adonis said Artist Records want to sign me, but it will take a few months before I can get an advance. What the fuck am I supposed to do until then? Starve?"

"Word! And when you get on, you can still have drugs on the block."

"I don't know about all that. If my album blows, I won't need to sell drugs." PT shook his head in agreement. "You're going to be with me anyway. You know I can't perform without my hype-man."

"No doubt."

"Nut is supposed to front me an ounce so I can get on my feet." Rome paused to exhale the smoke. "We are going to bubble on Gates like old days."

Rome and PT grew up together on Gates Ave. Putting work on their old block would be easy. The only cat they had to watch out for was a guy from Quincy Ave who they had beef with back in the days. It was one of those beefs that created war stories in the hood. It was Gates Ave verses Quincy Ave.

A couple of guys got shot on Gates and on Quincy. What took the cake was when Awol from Gates shot Big Walt from Quincy. Big Walt was in the middle of the street screaming at the top of his lungs for his mother. Everyone thought for sure he was a goner.

The beef between Gates and Quincy eventually died out, but old beef was known to get cooking in Brooklyn. All it took was something like what Rome and PT were about to do.

The next day Rome and PT set up shop on Gates, between Marcus Garvey and Troop. It was moving slowly on the first day. By the third day, all of the fiends knew that they had it good on Gates.

The Narcs were always easy to spot in Brooklyn; two White boys driving around in a funny looking car, in an all-Black neighborhood, looking at everyone suspiciously. And to top it off, they drove really slowly. That gave the dealers an advantage, but never sleep.

Business was going smoothly for the first two weeks. Rome paid Nut back for the ounce. Now he had two thousand dollars of his own. His initial plan was just to make enough money to buy his son and himself some things. Business was going so well that he made his mark and passed it.

Rome and PT were getting all the money. Customers even came from Quincy to cop from them. That didn't sit too well with Big Walt. Rome knew sooner or later, he would be getting a visit from Big Walt.

Ever since Big Walt got shot on Gates, he had a personal vendetta against anyone from Gates. Big Walt would often intimidate the younger dudes from Gates. Most of them were too young to know about the beef that happened in the past. That's why Big Walt got shot in the first place; he was being a bully. He was always big for his age. He liked to push his weight around, not anticipating that someone could clap his big ass.

The day finally came when Big Walt came strolling down Gates with two goons by his side. PT went to the stash to get the 9mm. Rome was serving a customer when Big Walt and his henchmen stopped where Rome was standing.

"What's good Rome?" Big Walt asked sarcastically.

"Ain't nothing, just doing me."

"I see you bubbling over here. Shit slowed down on my end."

"Sorry to hear that."

"Yeah, well, you are going to be real sorry if you don't take your show on the road," said Big Walt in an aggressive tone.

"Click-click!" Was the sound that stopped Big Walt's last words. The sound came from PT's gun that he now held at Big Walt's temple. "I dare one of you to act like you wanna reach. I'll blow you man's head off his shoulders."

Rome stuck his hand in the waist of both men and disarmed them of their weapons; a .357 magnum and the other was a .45 caliber. Rome put one of the weapons in his waist, and held the other one.

"You lucky we don't just clap all three of you right now," Rome said through clenched teeth. "You didn't learn your lesson the last time your big ass got clapped on Gates. Don't let me see you around here again." Rome dismissed them.

Big Walt and his henchmen ran off like three cowardly dogs with their tails tucked between their legs. Rome and PT scored a victory today. However, Rome knew that this wouldn't be the end of it. For sure, Big Walt would come back.

Business was going so well on the block that Rome got some workers. He and PT just sat on the block and supervised them. They were ready for Big Walt if he came back. All of them were strapped.

Rome got a call from Adonis while they were on the block. "What's really good, Adonis?"

"I have good news and bad news. Which one do you want first?"

"The bad news, I'm used to it."

"The bad news is that your album won't be released until late this year or next year. The good news is that Artist Records is ready to sign you to a three album deal."

Rome couldn't believe it. "Are you serious?"

"I don't joke about record deals. It's what I do."

"When do I sign?"

"Next week."

"So when can I get a signing bonus?"

"I'm working on that. We should be able to get you 10% of the $300,000 budget; about $30,000."

Rome raised his eyebrows. His mind quickly calculated what he could do with the money. "That sounds good. I'll be at the office ASAP." Rome hung up.

Rome told PT the news. He asked PT to hold down the block while he went to the office to get his contract. Things were looking really good for Rome. He was very excited, though he didn't show it. This was the moment of his life. He had waited twelve years for this. He thought about how he was going to floss once he made lots of money

Rome fantasized about being a celebrity, hearing his songs on the radio, and seeing his face on the TV. All these thoughts were entering his mind at once.

He even thought about how he was going to look out for PT. Rome had lots of love for PT. PT was a thorough soldier. He would kill for Rome and vice versa. Now it was their time to shine.

Meanwhile, back on Quincy Ave., Big Walt was getting a plan together to take out Rome and PT once and for all. He had been devising a master plan from the day PT put the gun to his head. He thought about just going back and blazing it out like the westerns. He knew Rome and PT would be on point for that type of retaliation. Big Walt knew they had recruited reinforcements. It took him two weeks to come up with a final plan that would be a perfect sneak attack on them.

Big Walt knew of two gun busting chicks from Flatbush who made a name for themselves. They were contract killers. They were known as Cagney & Lacey, named after the popular 80's TV series about two female gun-toting detectives.

Cagney & Lacey had a notorious reputation for setting up big time drug dealers. Then they graduated to being contract assassins. In Brooklyn, people in the streets referred to them as two Thorough Bitches.

Big Walt went to Flatbush to find Cagney & Lacey. They moved around a lot because of their dangerous endeavors. They would be hard to find because no one knew what they really looked like. They always wore a disguise. After a couple of days of inquiring, Big Walt finally found a way to contact them. There was a girl named Tamika who was their contact. He got Tamika's address through a reliable source.

Big Walt buzzed the bell to apartment 5A. A childlike voice came over the intercom. "Who is it?"

"It's me, Big Walt. I called about you know who."

"Well, you're going to have to wait because I'm busy right now."

"I got two hundred dollars that says you can put that on hold." There was a short pause and then the door buzzed for him to enter.

He went to the elevator and rode it to the fifth floor. Before he could knock, the door opened. Tamika was a medium height, brown skinned girl. She was petite, but she had a little bubble of a butt. She had a short blond hair cut. She came to the door wearing a Chinese robe.

Her living room smelled like Budussy, a mixture of butt and pussy. There was some slow music playing on the stereo. Sex was definitely in the air. Tamika's boyfriend must be in the room, Walt thought.

"First things first." She stuck out the palm of her hand. "My two hundred."

Big Walt rolled his eyes and took a deep breath before digging into his pocket. He peeled off two crisp big face hundred dollar bills and placed them in her palm. She put the bills into the square pocket of her robe.

She grabbed a cordless phone from the wall and quickly dialed the number. "Hello, Cagney. A guy is here to talk to you." There was a short pause. "Twenty minutes, OK." Tamika hung up the phone. "She said she will be here in twenty minutes." She reached into her robe pocket and pulled out a glass jar. "Here... In the meantime, roll up a blunt."

Big Walt rolled up the blunt and lit it. He took two pulls and passed it to Tamika. Tamika took two and called her friend to come out and smoke some.

When Big Walt saw who came out of the room, he choked to keep from laughing. It was a girl. Tamika was a lesbian. That's why the apartment smelled like vagina, he thought to himself.

"Yeah, I'm gay, and what?" She spoke like she was at a gay pride convention.

"Hey, do your thing ma."

By the time they were finished smoking the blunt, Tamika's buzzer rang. "Who is it?" asked Tamika.

"It's me."

Tamika buzzed in the familiar female voice. When Cagney entered the apartment, you could tell she was wearing a disguise. She wore an auburn colored wig with black glasses, high heel shoes, and a black leather trench coat. It definitely wasn't summer wear.   She looked ridiculous and was very visibly nervous.

The first thing Cagney did was pull out some kind of device the size of a beeper. Then she told Big Walt to stand up. She ran the device over his whole body. It had a bug detector to make sure he wasn't working with the cops. Cagney and her partner, Lacey, were wanted. Not only by the cops, but also by drug dealers they robbed. The only good thing was that the cops had no positive ID on them or their real names.

"OK Mr. Walt, what can I do for you?"

"I have these two little cockroaches that I need exterminated."

"I see. And where are these cockroaches at?"

"They're on Gates, between Troop and Marcus Garvey."

"OK. For two, I'm going to charge you ten thousand, and I want half up front."

"I'll give you $7,500. Take it or leave it." Cagney thought about the price and agreed. "When do you want it done?"

"As soon as possible."

"It will take me at least two days to prepare. You do have pictures of my targets?"

"No, I don't, but it won't be hard to spot them."

"Now you're talking about a couple extra days, a week at the most."

"I'm losing money every day they're alive." Big Walt spoke desperately.

"All right, pay me and we'll case the area, get an ID of our targets, and do the hit."

Big Walt gave Cagney $3,500 cash up front. He was a cheap guy, so it hurt him to part with it. He thought of it as an investment. Once they were gone, his pockets will be right again.

"Your little problems are dead men walking." Cagney spoke with the seriousness of a veteran killer.

She gave Big Walt a cell number to contact her. She left the apartment without a word.

Big Walt liked the way Cagney did business. When you want the best, you have to pay for it, he thought to himself.

"We'll see who gets the last laugh," Walt said to himself as he exited the building.

CHAPTER 4

It had been almost two weeks since Monica met Adonis and gave him her numbers. She hadn't heard from him, which was unusual for Monica since no man has ever gotten her number and not called her. I gave him two numbers, she thought. She anticipated his call every day. Now she was in FUCK ADONIS mode. I have too many men to worry about one man, she thought to herself

"Oh well, it's his loss, not mine," she said to herself as she got immaculately dressed. She had a date with one of her favorite tricks. He was a rap star named Official. Monica met him at Sue's. At the time, he had the number one song in the country. His videos were in heavy rotation, and everyone bumped his songs in their cars. Monica loved to dance to Official's songs.

The night he came into the club, Official acted like he had never seen a woman as beautiful as Monica. He offered to pay her to leave with him. She told him she could make $1,500 if she stayed. He gave her $2,500 and they drove off in his CLS 500 Benz.

Monica liked the attention she got from being with Official. He was a funny character to her. However, he was nothing like his music suggested. On all of his records, he bragged about how big his dick was and how much of a pimp he was. He rapped about how ghetto he is because he grew up in Brooklyn. If you let him tell it, he was the realest gangsta in the industry.

The truth is, Official was the opposite of everything he rapped about. He had a little dick and he suffered from premature ejaculation. He was far from being a pimp or a player; actually, he was getting played. He spent over $25,000 on Monica alone, not counting all of the other girls that he tricked on.

He grew up in Brooklyn, but not in the ghetto part. He grew up in a nice, clean, upper middle class neighborhood in Williamsburg. His family was a replica of the Huxtables. His father was a doctor and his mother was a lawyer.

Regardless of his shortcomings, Monica liked his company. He was a nice guy; he treated her like a Queen. Whenever Monica wanted to feel like a celebrity outside the club, she called Dexter. Dexter was Official's government name. Dexter Ring Wald Tremont, the third. Monica thought Dexter was comical. She would tell Trina stories about him and she had jokes for days about him.

The funniest one was the first time Monica had sex with Official. She just knew from listening to his songs that he was going to do his thing. He worked out, so he had a six pack and muscles everywhere. From the outside, he was packing.

He started out good, with lots of foreplay, licking and touching. He performed oral sex on Monica. The things he was saying even turned her on.

"I'm going to wear this pussy out." He promised.

"Yeah daddy! Fuck me!"

Dexter got on top in a position to penetrate. Monica had a habit of closing her eyes until she felt the penis inside. She had her eyes closed for two minutes before she heard him say, "I'm coming!"

He rolled over. "That was good."

"It was, wasn't it?"

The worst thing you could do to a horny Black Woman is to fail in satisfying her. She would have been mad if it wasn't for the 3 carat ring Official bought her earlier that day.

Trina thought that story was hilarious. "Mr. Big shot rapper with his little dick," Trina said laughing. "Don't worry; your little secret is safe with me. Get it? Little secret." After each joke came more laughter.

That night, Monica and Official were attending an album release party. Official liked to bring Monica to events like this and Monica liked to be seen with him. She didn't even charge him for his time. She didn't have to because he always bought her an expensive outfit.

Official pulled up in front of Monica's condo and beeped his horn. He drove a house on wheels. The price could buy someone a mini mansion. Official drove a $250,000 2010 Bentley Flying Spur. Just the thought of being in a Bentley excited Monica. She finished the last touches on her outfit and strolled to the passenger side of the Bentley.

They were on the VIP list, so they didn't have to wait on line. The world famous Biz Markie was on the wheels of steel. The place was packed.

Official and Monica went straight to the VIP. Walking through the crowd of Official fans was sometimes annoying to Monica. She never got used to how people would react when they saw him.

"Look! There goes Official!" A crazed fan shouted, almost causing a riot. A bodyguard made a path for them.

When they made it to the VIP room, things calmed down. The VIP consisted of mostly label execs and artist. They were not in VIP for five minutes before Monica spotted Adonis. Adonis and Rome were mingling with some slim model-type chicks.

Her first thought was to avoid seeing him, and then she changed her mind. She wanted to be seen. Being seen with an important person like Official should make him jealous, she thought.

It so happened that Official and Adonis knew each other. As Monica and Official moved towards the bar, Official stopped in front of Adonis and said, "What up Adonis?" like they were best friends. "Hey, we still on for some hoops this weekend?"

"No question."

Adonis had noticed Monica standing with Dexter. He had a look of surprise on his face. She was the most startling woman in the entire V.I.P. Adonis began staring at Monica. Dexter noticed the look of familiarity on Monica and Adonis' faces.

"How're you doing, Monica?" Adonis asked.

"Adonis, I'm fine, how about you?"

"I could be better."

Dexter rudely interjected. "So, you two know each other?"

"Yeah, I met Monica a few weeks ago at a birthday party."

"So, you know my boo?" said Dexter as he pulled Monica closer to him, a fake gesture of them being lovers. Monica slightly pulled away and made a face that said, "No, I'm not your boo," without saying a word.

Adonis picked up on the vibe Monica was giving off and Dexter also picked up on Monica's resistance. Dexter was fuming mad. He didn't like the way she was acting one bit.

"Excuse me, Adonis," Dexter said, grabbing Monica hard by her wrist. He dragged her to an empty corner, so no one could hear them.

"Listen, you fucking no good tramp. Don't you ever embarrass me like that again! Bitch, I own you! All of the things that I have given you and this is how you show your gratitude?" Dexter was visibly upset. "I'm Official, you understand me? I can have any bitch out here!" He finally stopped ranting to catch his breath.

Now it was Monica's turn. He had really done it this time. He was going to be sorry he ever met her after tonight. The Bedford-Stuyvesant,   Brooklyn was about to come out of her.

"Let me tell you something, you fake ass, little dick, corny motherfucker! You don't own me. I've been playing your dumb ass since day one. You're nothing but a sorry ass trick!" Monica screamed with fire in her voice. "Don't forget...I know who you really are. A little dick trick from Williamsburg named Dexter Ring Wald Tremont, the Third. I will go to every tabloid, rap magazine, MTV, BET, VH1, even Oprah, and tell the world the truth about you." Monica spoke like a women scorned. "And furthermore, fuck you! I'll find my own way home!" Then she walked away from him.

Adonis and Rome watched the whole exchange unfold from across the room. They weren't close enough to hear the disagreement, but could tell from the body language that the conversation was argumentative. Monica left Dexter standing there. That display summed it up.

As Monica walked pass Adonis, he called her name. She turned to see who was calling her. "Are you leaving so soon?" asked Adonis.

"Yes I'm leaving. Why?" Monica replied in an aggravated tone.

"But you just got here. I saw what happened with your date, Dexter. Since I'm here alone, I was thinking that maybe I could be your date for the remainder of the night?"

"You don't even know how to call nobody," Monica said in a frustrated manner.

"I'm sorry; it's just that I've been so busy lately. Every time I make a mental note to call you, something else comes up. I still have your numbers." His boyish face made his apology sweet and sincere. Monica could not resist his offer.

Adonis and Rome had their own table in the V.I.P. room; Rome had a girl with him at the table. Monica looked at her with a familiar expression. Monica thought she had seen this girl somewhere before. Rome and Adonis had two bottles of Moet Rosé chilling on ice. When Monica focused on Rome's date, she remembered who the female was. She was Tamya, the R&B singing sensation. Rome is moving up in the world, Monica thought. A step above the hood rats he usually cheated on Trina with.

"We are having a little celebration of our own." announced Adonis as he poured four glasses of Rose`. "Here's a toast to newly signed Artist Records recording artist, Rome." They gave a toast and drank from their glasses.

"Congratulations, Rome. You deserve it," said Monica.

"Thank you, Monica. It's been a long time coming, but a change is going to come." Rome replied like he just won a game.

Adonis and Monica sat closer to each other. They both had that strange feeling that two people get on their first date. To break the ice, Adonis said, "Well, how do you know Dexter? He is a pretty popular guy."

"I knew him before he was Mr. Official. He is really very conceited now that he has a little fame. I'd rather not speak about him."

Adonis began thinking of another topic to speak on. Before he decided on a subject, Monica had a question of her own for him.

"Your daughter, are you still with her mother?" A sad expression consumed Adonis' face as he thought of his child's mother. Monica observed this drastic change in Adonis' affect.

"I'm sorry if I'm getting too personal," said Monica.

Adonis stopped her before she could begin another sentence. "No, it's all right. It's just that my wife was killed in a car accident a year ago." Monica's face showed genuine concern.

"I'm sorry to hear that."

"It's ok; I have no choice but to be strong for my daughter. Life has to go on."

This topic changed the whole vibe that they shared prior to her mention of his deceased wife. Monica had an idea to return the mood to a party one. She grabbed Adonis by the hand and said, "Come on let's get our groove on!"

"I really don't know how to dance."

"Don't worry, I'll show you."

They got up and proceeded to the dance floor. Monica considered herself a professional dancer. Even though she took no formal dance lessons, all of the hours she spent as an exotic dancer had to account for something, she figured.

When they got on the dance floor, Biz Markie was taking it back in the days, to the old school. The old songs always get the crowd hyped up. The dance floor was packed. The hottest songs from the late 80's and 90's had Monica shaking her big rump like she was going to break something.

Adonis could not help but get into the music. He did a simple two step that most non-dancers do. Monica danced in circles around Adonis. She attracted lots of attention. Guys were staring at her with lustful eyes. Adonis liked the extra attention that this beautiful female specimen attracted. He was turned on.

Monica then did something that aroused Adonis so much that he became erect instantly. Monica's intentions to entice Adonis now became clear. She turned her back towards him, grabbed his hands and placed them on her hips. Then she grinded her big soft buttocks into his penis in a gyrating motion. Adonis had not had sex since his wife was killed. His reaction to how Monica danced on him was causing a great sensation. He started unintentionally humping her buttocks. She responded with more rump shaking movements that were driving Adonis crazy.

Monica could feel the size of his manhood through his silk slacks. From her experience at lap dancing, Monica could figure out how big the clients' packages were. In this case, she could tell that Adonis would put

Dexter to shame in the size department. She even started to get moist from all the dancing.

Then something happened to Adonis before he had any control to stop it. He was so into the grinding and pumping actions of their erotic dancing that he ejaculated in his boxer shorts. Since he was so backed up from a year of celibacy, he had a load. There was enough sperm in his boxers to fill up a shot glass. It was all oozing down his leg. He almost lost his balance and fell to the side, but he caught himself.

"Excuse me, Monica. I have to use the bathroom," Adonis said, interrupting Monica's dancing.

Monica had a feeling that he would get hard. The way he ran off to the bathroom told her that he did more than just get erect.

When Adonis got to the bathroom, all of the stalls were full. The sticky semen was now dripping down into his socks. He was starting to feel the side effects of having an orgasm. Adonis was relaxed and calm as if he took sedation pills.

Finally, a stall opened. When he pulled his slacks down, he noticed he was still dripping semen from his penis. He took a glob of tissue and wiped his legs and the inside of his boxer shorts. He wanted to go home, but he decided not to spoil the night. Besides, the club was so hot that he'd be dry within an hour.

When Adonis returned to their table, he saw that Monica was still on the dance floor. Some guy was dancing with her. Adonis was pleased that she wasn't giving him the treat that she gave Adonis. He poured a glass of Rose` and guzzled it. Then he poured another one. He was watching Monica dance. Her every move was graceful, sensual, and sexy. He could tell that she had lots of practice. She was enjoying herself.

Monica glanced over at the table and saw Adonis looking at her. She took the opportunity to do one of her signature moves. She dipped her ass low to the floor, then she wiggled it and shook her breast on the way up; this was one of her signature moves from her job.

Adonis continued to be turned on by her seductive moves. With the Rose˘ setting in, his character was starting to transform. He drank the entire bottle of Rose˘. Adonis wasn't a drinker, so he was already feeling drunk.

Monica stopped dancing and made her way over to sit with Adonis. The guy she was dancing with kept trying to get her number. He was the type to brag about his accomplishments.

"I'm the CEO of Top Cat records, baby," he professed. All Monica saw was a trick to be played. He looked like he had money from all the diamonds he wore. Luckily for him, she wasn't here for business.

When she got to the table, she noticed the look on Adonis' face. He was drunk. Monica saw the empty bottle of Rose˘ and knew what it was.

The rest of the night was like an interview with a drunken man. You know, when a person gets drunk and they talk a lot, usually they tell the truth.

"I really like you," Adonis slurred. "Really, ever since I met you, I-I liked you. You are so pretty, just like my Tammy." Adonis became overwhelmed with emotions. "I really miss Tammy. I'm so lonely. Will you be my friend?" Adonis spoke in a drunken stupor.

"Yes, I'll be your friend," Monica said, holding Adonis's head up to her breast while rubbing his curly hair.

As Rome and Tamya got up to leave, he decided to give Monica the keys to Adonis' Range Rover. He asked her to take Adonis to her condo. His daughter was spending the night at Trina's house.

When Adonis woke up the next day, it was already the afternoon. He didn't know where he was, or what happened. He couldn't remember anything about last night. He looked over and saw Monica standing there, holding a breakfast tray.

"I made you eggs, English muffins and some pancakes." There was also some freshly squeezed orange juice.

Adonis had a serious hangover. "What happened last night?" He noticed he was in her bed. "Did we...?"

"No, we didn't. You did what people normally do when they're drunk. You just talked a lot."

Adonis felt relieved that he didn't do anything he would regret. He ate the breakfast that Monica made for him, which made him feel much better.

"Thank you for the breakfast and everything."

"Mm-hmm, don't mention it." Monica responded nonchalantly. "I have some brand new boxers and t-shirts your size. You can take a shower before you go to pick up your daughter."

Adonis took a shower and got dressed. When he was about to leave, Monica stopped him at the door.

"Aren't you forgetting something?"

He stopped and thought about it. She walked up to him and threw her arms around his neck and French kissed him seductively. It was the most passionate kiss that Adonis ever had.

"Don't forget to call me this time."

"How can I forget to call when I won't be able to think about anything else but you?"

Monica was very pleased with his response. She was surer now that Adonis was interested in her. She was more than just interested in Adonis; she was in Love. She just didn't know it yet.

CHAPTER 5

Rome and PT were moving up fast in the drug game. When Rome got signed, Adonis was able to get him an early signing bonus. He got $20,000. Not what he expected, but it beats a blank. He took half of that and bought a quarter of a kilo. He tripled his money in a week. Rome and PT had all the customers buying from them. Big Walt was hurting.

Rome left PT in charge of the spot while he was in the studio. When he wasn't in the studio, he was on the block. Rome copped a new Cadillac Escalade. His new girlfriend, Tamya --the R&B singer from the party-- drove a S600 Benz. He drove the Benz, too. He was living the life he always dreamed about. What he didn't know was that he had a hit out on him.

Cagney and Lacey had been coming through the block, buying crack from Rome's spot. They pretended to be crack heads to get familiar with their dealers. They were stalling on the hit because they wanted to get Rome and PT together at the same time. Rome hardly came to the spot anymore because of the studio. Today was different.

They spotted the Black Escalade on Gates Ave. They knew they were both there today. They had to get the job over with because Big Walt was getting impatient. He complained to Cagney every day about how he was losing money.

"Get them this week or give me back my money!" Walt protested.

It was going down today. Even if they just got one, they had to put that work in. They cocked back their weapons and took off the safeties. Cagney and Lacey liked to carry big guns. Cagney had a .40 caliber and Lacey had a Desert Eagle. They both had extra clips, just in case. Rome and PT's fate was now in their hands.

Two workers and PT were standing around the truck listening to Rome's music. They weren't paying attention to the two females walking up the block.

Cagney and Lacey walked up the block and one of the workers recognized them as customers. As he walked towards them to serve them, he saw them both pulling out their weapons.

He yelled, "Get Down!" Before pulling out a .380 caliber pistol.

It was too late. They already began to let off rounds from their cannons. BOOM! BOOM! BOOM!

As they shot their weapons, they walked forward like two killer robots. The young soldier that gave the warning was the first one to get hit. The impact of the big slugs knocked him ten feet back.

PT pulled out his gun and rapidly emptied the first clip. PT hit Cagney in the chest three times. Lacey hit PT twice, once in the neck and once in the head. Fragments of his skull splattered on the side of Rome's Escalade. Rome knew for sure that PT was a goner.

The other worker picked up the abandoned .380 and let off the remaining rounds. He hit Lacey once in the shoulder. People were screaming and ducking everywhere.

Rome rolled under the truck to the other side. He was out of the killer's sight.

Both Cagney and Lacey had on Bullet proof vests. The three slugs that hit Cagney still knocked her unconscious. Lacey had a shoulder wound. She was losing lots of blood but she didn't want to leave without her partner.

"Cagney, get up! Don't get soft on me now!" Lacey was trying to revive her partner. Cagney didn't respond. She was out cold from the impact of the slugs to her chest. The slugs didn't penetrate her vest but they still damaged her.

Sirens were sounding very close. Rome got into his truck and sped off. Lacey was getting weak from losing blood. She was too weak to run. She walked a block and entered a Bodega. "Please help me! Call an ambulance, I'm shot," Lacey begged.

The owner just looked at her like she was crazy. She was still holding the desert eagle in her hand, which frightened the owner. When she noticed why he was just standing there, she stuck the gun to his head.

"Stupid motherfucker! Call the damn ambulance!"

The police arrived on the scene and saw a trail of blood on the concrete. They followed it into the Bodega. When they opened the door, they saw a woman holding a gun to the owner's head. "FREEZE! Drop the weapon!" one of the officers yelled.

Lacey made the fatal mistake of turning the gun towards the police officers. The next thing you heard was a barrage of gunfire. Lacey was hit so many times that her body shook like she was doing the Harlem shake. She was shot 21 times.

Cagney was taken in the ambulance. Someone had picked up her .40 caliber, so there was no weapon on the scene. No one cooperated with the cops, so they didn't know Cagney was the culprit in the crime. As far as they knew, she was an innocent bystander caught in the crossfire; it happens all the time in Brooklyn.

The only question that the cops had was why she was wearing a bullet proof vest. Whatever the reason, one cop thought, it saved her life.

Cagney would be in the hospital for a day or two. They wouldn't release her until they were sure she was back to normal health.

Meanwhile, homicide detectives Anthony Brown and Vincent Santiago needed some answers. Detectives Brown and Santiago were hot on the trail of Cagney and Lacey. Although they had no positive ID or fingerprints on them, the detectives knew they existed.

Did they? Maybe they were just legends, another story told in the naked city. No one had any real proof that they were real people because no one could say how they looked. There were people who met one but couldn't describe her if you paid them to. So, except for word of mouth, there was no real proof except for one deceased old lady.

The old lady was a witness to suspects in a robbery and murder case. She saw two women fleeing the building. They were both wearing wigs. She couldn't give any better description than that, but that was good enough.

Brown had heard that they always wore wigs as a disguise. That was his proof that they were real people. The old lady died shortly after the crime. Ever since then, Brown was obsessed with catching them.

Brown and Santiago were at the scene of the murder to investigate. "Twenty-four year old Antwon Johnson and a sixteen year old, James Hightower, are the two victims." Santiago reported. "Gun powder residue was on both of the victims hands, which confirms that they fired weapons. There were no guns found at the scene. No witnesses, typical of neighborhoods like these."

Brown assessed the information. "The only lead is the murdered woman in the Bodega and the innocent bystander?" Brown thought. He believed in the notion that something wasn't right.

"We need to take a look at the body before they cart it off," Brown ordered.

Santiago stopped the ambulance. He opened the back door. The two detectives got in the ambulance. Brown unzipped the body bag and saw a fairly young Black woman. The sight of her bullet riddled body was grotesque.

"Look, she has on a wig," Santiago said.

Instinctively, Brown checked to see if the woman was wearing a bullet proof vest. Just as his intuition told him, she was wearing one. They both looked at each other as if they were telepathically speaking.

"Bingo! A thousand dollars says that our so-called innocent bystander down at Kings County had on a wig and a vest also." Brown spoke like the host of a game show.

"We may just have our female assassins."

Brown immediately called Kings County Hospital. A receptionist answered, "Kings County, may I help you?"

"Yes, this is Detective Brown from the 81st. A black woman was admitted from a shootout on Gates."

"Yes, I'm familiar with that victim."

"Could you forward this call to the room of the victim?"

The nurse routed the call to the room Cagney was in. A nurse picked up.

"Listen carefully. Does the injured woman have on a wig and a bullet proof vest?" Brown inquired.

"Yes, she does have on a wig. We removed the vest. Lucky for her, she had it on."

"Thank you." Brown hung up the phone. He didn't want to alert the nurse any more than he had. He and Santiago were going to race to the hospital themselves and apprehend their mystery woman.

When the nurse hung up, she didn't know that Cagney heard every word that was said. Cagney was no longer unconscious. She was in a lot of pain, but she would live. Now she knew she had to get out of there fast.

The nurse left the room. Now was Cagney's only chance to slip out of the hospital. She had no time to be a sucker for pain. She put on her clothes and walked out of the room. Just as Cagney turned the corner, the nurse was entering the room. The nurse ran out of the room looking for Cagney. The doors from the elevator closed just before the nurse could see Cagney get on it.

When Cagney got to the ground floor, she quickly flagged a cab. "Take me to Avenue A in Flatbush." The cab drove off.

As Cagney's cab was pulling off from the curb, Detectives Brown and Santiago were pulling up to the hospital. They quickly hopped out of their car and ran to the reception desk and got the room number to Cagney's room. When they got to the room, the nurse was standing

46

there holding the hospital gown and the wig that Cagney wore. The mystery woman had vanished into thin air.

CHAPTER 6

Rome drove straight to his private parking garage, and then he called his new girlfriend, Tamya. He told her to come and pick him up. She was there within an hour.

Rome was hysterical. He had just seen his best friend's brains splattered on his truck. He knew who was responsible for all of this; none other than Big Walt himself.

When Tamya reached the garage, she noticed right away that something was wrong. Rome was sweating and pacing when she pulled up to the curb.

"What's wrong baby?"

"Two chicks just blew my best friend's brains out. They were gunning for me, too."

Rome turned on the news on her TV in the car. Sure enough, the reporter was on the scene covering the event that just occurred.

"Twenty-four year old Antwon Johnson and another sixteen year old Black male, whose name we cannot mention because of his age, were gunned down this afternoon. One witness said two females are responsible for the shooting. One of the females was gunned down by NYPD in a bodega half a block from the incident. The gunwoman was identified as twenty-seven year old Stacey Jenkins." Rome abruptly turned off the TV.

They drove to Tamya's midtown Manhattan penthouse. Rome needed to relax, so he got into the Jacuzzi, puffed on a blunt, and sipped on some Henny. Thoughts were racing through his mind. He wanted to kill fat ass Big Walt himself. He knew at this point that would destroy his career. If anything, I'll get someone else to do it for me, he thought.

He thought about all the plans he had for him and PT once he got on. They talked about going on tour, getting money, and sexing groupies. Without PT, he had no one left. All his other friends were in jail, or dead. All that was left of the original team was him and PT. Now PT was gone.

"When will the drama end?" he asked himself. Blacks killing each other, dying over streets that we don't even own. Was it all really worth it?

Rome thought deeply. Was all the drama just an illusion? One thing was for sure, the streets will promise you death or prison and sometimes both.

He thought about how close he came to losing his life today, just when he was about to drop an album to let the world hear his story. This was the wake-up call for Rome. He was blessed to have a chance to change his life for the better. The streets almost took his chance. He thought about how stupid he was for being involved with selling drugs. I could have gone down for that stupid shit, he thought. Everyone was telling on each other. The game is not worth it.

He looked over at his beautiful new girlfriend, whom he really cared for. He thought: Would she do a bid with me? Not with a bright career, and so much going for her.

It's time for me to hang it up. The streets are not for me anymore. There are bigger and better things in my life.

"Fuck Big Walt! He can have that drug bullshit. He will get his, though." Rome shed tears as he spoke. He poured some Henny into the tub. "This is for you, PT. I'll never forget you." He smoked the rest of his blunt and dozed off in the Jacuzzi.

The next day, Rome told Adonis what happened. Adonis warned Rome about hanging out in the streets. Now it was time for him to play big brother.

"Look, Rome, you're a professional artist now. How many times do I have to tell you to stay out of the streets? We can't afford to have you shot or locked up."

"You right man. I'm done with the streets. I'm going to stay here at Tamya's for a while."

"We have studio appointments all week. So get ready."

"I got some shit I just wrote for PT that I want to lay down."

"You can do whatever. Just make hits so we can get this money."

"No doubt," said Rome.

Adonis always had a way to motivate his artists to do their best. Rome was happy that he met Adonis. Rome didn't believe in things happening by coincidence or chance. He believed that everything happened for a reason. It was destiny that Rome performed at Speed that night. He remembered not wanting to do the show that night, but his man talked him into it. Something inside him told him to just go. The rest is history.

Monica heard about what happened to PT on Gates Ave. She grew up with PT. They all went to school together: Monica, Trina, Rome and PT. She cried all morning when she heard about PT's murder. She felt for the young boy, also. Monica didn't have any children. She could only imagine what it must feel like to lose a child. Growing up in the ghetto, you see death so much it starts to become normal. Inside, you know it is not normal. You just pretend that it is normal for your own sanity. The same way a soldier in a war has to trick his mind into believing it's his duty to kill. There is a war on the streets, with casualties every day. The sad part about it, Monica thought, was how Blacks are killing each other. As she thought, her phone rang.

"What's up girl?" Trina asked in a monotone of sadness.

"I'm just chilling, sitting here thinking about how shit is fucked up for Black people in this world," Monica replied in the same tone.

"I guess you heard about PT."

"I just saw him three days ago. He was looking good. You know I used to like him back in the day."

"I remember when you gave him the name Pretty Twon." Trina smiled at the thought.

"That name stuck with him. I remember he didn't like that name at first. I guess it just grew on him," Monica said while having flashbacks.

"You know Rome was there when it happened. He said the two chicks were trying to kill him, too." Trina paused before saying her next words. "Don't say anything, but Rome said Big Walt from Quincy Ave put a hit out on him and PT."

"Word! Big Walt is a bitch. I remember when his bitch ass got shot on Gates and he was calling his mother."

"I just hope Rome doesn't go get himself in trouble over this shit."

"I know. He just got signed. That's all he needs is a murder charge and its over for him." Monica's phone was beeping, indicating that a call was waiting. "Hold on Trina, someone is calling on the other line." Monica pressed a button, "Hello."

"Monica, this is Adonis. What are you doing today?" he asked.

"Nothing really, I was just talking to Trina about PT."

"How would you like to have lunch with me today?"

"Sure. You want to pick me up, or would you like to meet somewhere?"

"I'll come and get you at 12:30. How does that sound?"

"That's perfect."

"See you then." Adonis hung up. Monica clicked back over to Trina.

"Trina, guess who that was?"

"I don't fucking know, Publishing Clearing House?" Trina answered sarcastically. "Who was it?"

"It was Adonis. He asked me out to lunch today!" Monica said the words like the winner of a contest.

"At least one of us is getting some play. I haven't had any dick in months. I'm about to get a vibrator. Fuck a man! At least a vibrator won't cheat or lie."

"Well, let me go get ready for my date. I'll call you later and give you all the details."

The call from Adonis boosted Monica's spirits. Before he called, she was sad from grieving over PT's death. She was energized now and anxious to see Adonis.

Monica chose a relaxed, casual look for her lunch date with Adonis. She didn't want to look too seductive as it was only lunch. At the same time, she wanted to look sexy by wearing something that would accentuate her curves. She chose a Gucci outfit with some Gucci sandals. The pants and shirt were form fitting, so her butt looked marvelous.

It was something about a nice ass that drove Black men wild. A chick could be ugly as hell, with no chest. But if she had a big ass, a Black Man is going to want her. In Monica's case, she had the total package.

Adonis was five minutes early or maybe his watch was just five minutes faster. Monica liked a man who was on time. Most men were always late, at least, so it seemed to Monica. One point for Adonis, she thought to herself.

When she came out of her condo, Adonis stepped out of his Range Rover and greeted her with a big hug and a kiss. He complimented her on her attire. Then he walked her to the passenger side door and opened it. He waited for her to be seated then he closed the door.

Adonis is such a gentleman, she thought. Two points for Adonis.

As they drove off, the car's system was playing some new music that Monica never heard before.

"I'm feeling this. Who is this singing?" It sounds like Grace."

"It is Grace's new album. I'm feeling it, too. I think she is going to go double platinum this time."

"Let me know when it comes out, so I can go cop it."

"You can have this one. The label gives me 100 free copies for promotion," said Adonis with a perfect smile.

Monica said, "Thank you."

"Don't mention it."

Adonis took her to Justin's, P. Diddy's famous restaurant. You could always find a celebrity or two eating there

Upon being seated, Monica spotted Official. He was dining with a beautiful Mulatto looking woman. She was petite, with big breasts. Her breasts were possibly implants because they didn't fit her small frame.

Official acknowledged Adonis and Monica. "What's up?" Dexter said in a cynical tone.

"What's up Official?" Adonis replied.

"How're you doing DEXTER?" Monica added emphasis on Dexter's name. She knew that would annoy him.

She did it as a reminder that if he says anything about her stripping, she would keep her promise. Seeing Official almost spoiled her appetite.

The waiter gave them their menus. Adonis ordered a Cesar salad, some French fries, and a tofu burger. He didn't eat red meat. Monica ordered a baked potato, a salad, and shrimp scampi.

While their orders were being prepared, Adonis started a conversation. "Did you know that in ancient Africa they worshipped the Black Woman as a Goddess?"

"No, I didn't. Tell me about it." Monica found this topic interesting.

"Well in ancient Khemet, known today as Egypt, they developed a culture based on the feminine principals of nature. To them, the Black Woman and the Earth were one and the same. They marveled at the fact that the woman gave birth in the same ways the Earth did. They saw that as a divine attribute, so they held their woman up in the highest of regards as a Goddess."

"Do they still worship the Black Woman today in Africa?"

"A lot has changed since those times. For one, Africa has been invaded and colonized by many foreign conquerors. The conquerors forced their religion and doctrines on the Africans. Their original culture faded somewhat, but they still managed to retain a portion of their ancient beliefs and customs." Adonis paused to see if she was receptive. The expression on her face said she was. "As a matter of fact, proof of Goddess worship still exists today in some countries. It is said that the Pope worships a statue called the Black Madonna and Child. That is a statue of the African Goddess Isis holding her son Horus. The statue is known around the world."

Monica had never been told such great knowledge about her African ancestors. Doorways in her mind immediately opened up to receive more of this knowledge. Monica was under the impression that all Africans were savages and contributed nothing to civilization. Most African-Americans were taught this lie, when --in fact-- Africans are the fathers and mothers of all civilization.

"Please tell me more, Adonis." Adonis smiled at her request. He loved to meet Black women who wanted to know their history.

"Do you know how to play chess?" Adonis asked.

"Yes, I learned how to play chess when I was in high school."

"Did you ever wonder why the Queen is the most powerful piece on the Chess board?"

"No, but I noticed that the Queen can move anywhere on the board, where the other pieces cannot. She is a dangerous bitch. Pardon my French."

"The reason why she is the most powerful moving piece is because Chess was created in Africa during the Matriarchal system. A Matriarchal system is when the woman has equal power in a society. During the time of Goddess worship, Africa was a Matriarchal society. They created a game based on their culture, a game in which the woman has power. In Europe, they developed a Patriarchal Society. That is when the man assumes all positions of power and all women are secondary; much like America and most European run countries. Europeans would not have created a game where a woman has power."

"Wow, you mean to tell me that there was a time in history when I would have ruled over a man?" She was a bit confused. "I need to study my history, my African history. Will you teach me?"

"I will teach you all that I know, in due time." Adonis cracked a smile which melted Monica.

She liked his response. It meant that he planned on spending time with her. She knew it was something about Adonis, other than his looks. One hundred points for Adonis, she said to herself.

Their food arrived and it was looking rather tasty. Monica usually picked at her food, but today she was starving. It was no time to act cute. She felt comfortable around Adonis. She dug into her plate with a vengeance.

Adonis did everything like he was Royal. He didn't eat his food fast like most men. He took his time, slowly chewing his food. Then the next slow bite, then he slowly chewed. It was almost annoying.

They ate their food while dabbling in small talk. When they were finished, Adonis had to go back to work. He took Monica home and promised her that he would finish giving her history lessons.

"If I'm not tired when I finish work, I'll stop by or call, and we can add on to the lesson," Adonis said, staring into her beautiful eyes.

"OK, just call to make sure I'm home. Thank you for the lesson and the lunch. I had a very nice time. I look forward to learning more from you, teacher." She smiled, and this time *he* melted.

"Don't mention it." He leaned over and kissed her on the lips. It was a wet kiss.

Monica felt the electricity between them. Just as she was beginning to become over aroused, Adonis stopped.

"Peace, my beautiful Black Goddess."

"Peace, my handsome King." She smiled and exited the vehicle.

"What a man," Monica said to herself as Adonis drove off. She wanted to make him her man. It wasn't official yet, but things were looking good. The first date was a success. She didn't count the night at the club.

Monica knew she had issues to sort out before she got serious with Adonis. For one, he thinks I'm a model, but I'm a stripper, she thought. That makes me just as fraudulent as Dexter. These thought caused her stress.

Though she had a nice sized bank account, she also had an obsession for expensive things. She didn't feel right deceiving Adonis. She had to make a choice.

I will stop stripping once I know we're serious. What am I thinking? He is probably a lying, no-good dog, just like the rest of them. Just get what you can get out of him and keep it moving. But he is so intelligent and handsome. He is so different from other men. I'm going to give him a chance.

She lay on her bed and thought deeply about her and Adonis being together. She was confused. One part of her wanted to hold on to the game, but the other part of her wanted to change the game and settle down.

She called Trina to tell her about her date with Adonis. "What's up girl?" Monica said with cheer.

"The same shit that was up this morning, I'm horny, lonely and tired of no-good men."

"I just got back from my lunch date with Adonis. Let me tell you girl, homeboy is the one. I'm in love."

"Yeah, I bet. What makes him any different from the rest of the dog pack?"

"He is the first man that taught me anything about my African history. He is into that stuff real deep. He taught me how Black women were Goddesses. How we use to rule and oh man, it was just so deep." She spoke with so much enthusiasm that she was losing her breath. "He said he would teach me everything he knows, which means he plans on spending time with me. I could listen to him all day. He is so interesting the way he speaks, and the intense expression on his face."

"That sounds real deep. Ask him if he has a brother, or a cousin. Fuck it, a friend. I want to get my learning on too. That is, after we get our freak on."

"The only fucked up thing is that he thinks I'm a model for Fresh Faces. If he knew I was a stripper, I don't think he'd approve of it."

"Well, what are you going to do? I mean that stripper shit is getting played out."

"What you mean played out? It got me where I am. At least I'm not broke," Monica replied defensively.

"What you saying? I'm broke. Let me tell you something. I'd rather be broke than naked in front of one hundred horny men touching me and disrespecting me like a hoe."

Things were getting hot between the two of them now.

"Fuck you bitch. You just jealous because I got it all and you don't have shit. No one wants to fuck your sorry ass."

"At least I don't fuck the first ten men just because they'll give me money."

"Oh, it's like that. Fuck You!" Monica slammed the phone down as hard as she could.

Monica and Trina had many disagreements, but never this severe. Monica was fuming mad. She vowed never to speak to Trina again. That thought only lasted an hour. After she calmed down, she thought about everything Trina said. That had always been Trina's opinion of strippers.

Monica tried to get Trina to strip with her. Even then, she told Monica how she felt about that profession. Maybe Trina was right, Monica thought.

Monica had a different take on the subject. She wasn't ashamed of her body. She saw nothing wrong with getting money for just dancing. That was her logic.

There was a flip side and Monica knew what it was. She wasn't being real about it. The truth was that she stooped low for money. She wouldn't have sex for $100 like a lot of the other girls. Her magic number was $500. If you wanted to play, you had to pay. The principal remains the same. She was no different than a prostitute; she had sex for money.

Monica didn't like to look at it like that. Her love for materialism was stronger than her logical rational. She would often justify her actions by saying, "I don't have a man, and if a guy is going to give me $500 or better just for a taste, I'm going to take it."

It wasn't like she had a long line of customers paying $500 for her time. Most men preferred a $100 whore over a $500 one. The $100 whore was just as good. Monica liked to fool herself into believing that she wasn't a whore. You have to call a spade a spade.

She was getting a little tired of playing the game. When she thought about Adonis, she had a serious notion to stop. Adonis was the type of man she could see herself settling down with. Even though she was money hungry, she needed a significant other. Through all the stripping and getting money, all she wanted now was a man. She wanted that man to be Adonis.

Monica had a serious decision to make; either stop stripping or stop seeing Adonis. Or she could play the game and still try and develop a serious relationship with Adonis. She would like to have her cake and eat it too.

There was a chance that she could have the cake, but eating it too was another question.

CHAPTER 7

Rome's album was coming out better than expected. He put a great deal of time and energy into perfecting his lyrics. The A&R from the label thought Rome had the best rap album on Artist Records. The A&R rep even told Rome and Adonis he would try to see if he could get Rome's album release date moved up.

Since PT's murder, Rome changed. He didn't go to Gates Ave anymore; there was no need to. He had no family there, and Trina lived off of Fulton Ave.

He slowed down on drinking and smoking, too. He found out that he could write better music sober. He used to think that he had to be high to write good music.

He enjoyed his new outlook on life. He was starting to appreciate waking up to another day healthy and alive. He appreciated being able to have nice things. Rome was becoming a responsible man.

Adonis noticed the changed Rome. He and Rome became closer than ever. Rome saw how laid back and trouble free Adonis was. He adopted Adonis' principals in his own life. They played basketball every weekend, and video games every other day.

Adonis was thirty years old, five years older than Rome, who was 25. Those five years, coupled with Adonis' wisdom, made him wiser. Rome wanted to incorporate Adonis's demeanor into his own character.

Adonis was teaching Rome African history. Rome was really into the lessons Adonis was teaching him. Adonis gave him some introductory books to read, to get him familiar with African concepts and principals. He gave him *Worlds Great Men of Color* by J.A. Rogers, *They Came Before Columbus* by Ivan Van Sertima, and *Destruction of Black Civilization* by Chancellor Williams. Rome began to understand the importance of knowing your history.

"If you don't know your history, you don't know yourself. We are reflections of our ancestors. Without them, we wouldn't be here, so we pay homage to those before us," stated Adonis to Rome.

It all started to make sense. Rome started to realize that if more Black people knew their history, they would be more conscious. They would be proud to be Black. He was becoming more conscious as he learned.

Rome sat in a lounge chair contemplating his next move. A 60-inch plasma screen was playing music videos. Tamya's video came on while he was sitting. That's my baby girl, he thought to himself.

Tamya gyrated her young firm body to the rhythm of her hit single 'My Way'. She was the hottest R&B Diva in the industry. Rome knew that he was a lucky man to have a gem like Tamya.

Tamya's new album was number one on the charts. She was hot. Rome was very proud of her. He missed her, but he would have to get used to dating a celebrity.

Tamya's 23rd birthday was coming up on October 5th. Rome was going to surprise her and show up in St. Louis on one of her tour stops. He had a copy of her schedule. His plan was to fly out to St. Louis a day before and make the arrangements to be backstage waiting for her.

Rome couldn't wait to see the look on Tamya's face when she sees him. She had absolutely no idea about his

63

planned surprise. Rome was very anxious to be with Tamya on her birthday. They had only been dating for 3 months, but to Rome, it seemed like 3 years.

Tamya was the first woman that Rome didn't cheat on; not even once. Rome had a reputation with cheating. He felt bad about the way he cheated on Trina. He knew that Trina loved him very much. She would cry and beg him to be faithful, but then he would hurt her again.

If it wasn't for Monica convincing her to leave him, Trina would still be with him. Rome was content with his new arrangement with Tamya, so he was happy that Monica intervened.

Rome boarded a 7:00 pm flight to St. Louis. By the time he landed, Tamya's tour bus would be pulling into St. Louis. Setting up for the show would start at 3:00. The show starts at 7:00. Rome planned to be in Tamya's backstage dressing room.

The time finally came for Rome to hide in Tamya's dressing room. He noticed how big the Arena was. It held 50,000 people. He thought about the day when he would perform in front of this many people.

Rome met up with Frankie, the road manager. He was a 6'4 ex-college linebacker with a frame that said, "I'll BREAK you!"

"Rome, this way, her dressing room is back here. She should be here any minute. I called her to make sure she gets here on time," Frankie said in a deep tone.

"I can't wait to see the look on her face when she sees that I flew all the way out here for her birthday."

"You're a lucky man, Rome. Tamya is the sweetest, talented young star in the game."

"Thanks, man. I do feel good to have her." Rome had a half smile on his face. "Check this out." Rome handed Frankie a jewelry box. It was a platinum chain with a heart shaped medallion that had TAMYA in diamonds in the middle.

"Wow! That's some serious ice. Most have cost you a fortune."

"Nothing is too expensive for my baby girl."

"Here is her room. Nice meeting you, Rome. Tell Adonis he owes me one." Frankie walked away.

When he entered the dressing room, he decided to really surprise her by hiding in a costume rack in the corner. He would be out of sight when Tamya entered. Then he was going to pop out on her.

Rome looked at his watch. It was 2:35 and she was five minutes late. Just then, he heard Tamya's voice by the door. She was talking to someone, a guy.

Rome dashed to the costume rack and hid behind it. Rome peeked through a gold dress. What he saw next crushed him.

Tamya and her male companion entered the room together. When Rome focused on the guy, he knew who he was. Her companion was a well-known R&B singer named Authentic. He was a heart throb to women. His new album was already double platinum.

"What the fuck is he doing here?" Rome asked himself.

"You know I wasn't going to forget my baby's birthday," Authentic said as he romantically grabbed Tamya by the waist and kissed her.

"I'm so glad to see you, baby. I missed you so much. It's been almost three months since I last saw you."

Three months! That's how long I've been seeing her! Rome thought to himself.

"I'm going to be on the road touring for the rest of this year. Then I have a role in a movie. My schedule is packed." Authentic spoke nonchalantly. "Only reason I'm here today is because I just performed in the area last night. I figured I'd stay to see you. You think we have time for a quickie?"

"Why not? I want you so bad. Fuck me Authentic."

When Tamya said those words, Rome couldn't take it anymore. He burst out of his hiding spot like NYPD SWAT. Tamya and Authentic both looked at Rome with a surprised and shocked expression on their faces.

"Rome! What the fuck are you doing here?" Tamya yelled in a demanding voice.

"What the hell do you think I'm doing here? I came here to surprise you for your birthday, but I'm the one that got the surprise!"

Tamya just looked at him like he was stupid.

"Do you know this guy?"

"Yeah, he is a friend."

"Oh, I'm just a friend now. You wasn't saying that when you was sucking my dick."

"Rome, just go! Leave!"

As Rome was walking out of the room, he and Authentic caught eye contact.

"What the fuck are you looking at?" Authentic said in a threatening tone.

"Excuse me?" Rome heard exactly what he said. That was the set up.

"I said-"

"PONG!" was the sound of Rome's fist against Authentic's jaw. He was out cold on the couch.

Rome stood there for a few seconds waiting to see if he would get up. Authentic didn't budge. Rome looked at Tamya. His heart almost skipped a beat. He really liked her, and she was playing him. She didn't blink as she stared at Authentic laid out on the couch.

"Have a nice life," Rome said as he walked out of the room.

Rome was fortunate enough to catch the 4:30 flight back to New York.

Rome was deeply hurt. The one time that he didn't cheat was the first time *he* got cheated on. He thought he was in love with Tamya. Now that he thought about it, it was more lust than love. Just being with a Diva was a fantasy for any man.

He thought about Trina and his son while he was on the plane. For the first time, he understood how Trina felt when he always hurt her.

Trina was the only woman who truly loved Rome. She proved her love time after time. Rome really loved Trina, too. It was just a male ego trip he was going through with her. Most of the time, he did it just to see how many girls he could get.

Rome began to feel remorse for the way he treated Trina. He wanted to make it up to her. He was going to take the chain back to the jeweler and have them replace Tamya's name with the name Trina. It was the same number of letters.

Rome was going to reconcile with his son's mother. He thought about all the pain he caused her. This experience with Tamya taught him a lesson. The pain he felt in that dressing room was more than he could bear. He tried to imagine constantly going through this with someone he loved. For once, he felt sympathy for Trina.

Rome took out his cell phone and called Trina.

"Hello, Trina speaking."

"What's good Tee. I was thinking about you and, I just wanted to..." he paused before continuing. "I'm sorry for hurting you all these years. I know I've said sorry before, but I'm truly sincerely sorry for all the pain I caused you. I still love you and I will always love you."

Trina smiled on the other side of the phone. She knew that Rome loved her. She knew that one day he would grow up.

"I will always love you, Rome. Whenever you're ready to be the man I need you to be, the man that I know you can be, you are welcome back into our lives."

"I'm ready, Tee. This time let's take it one step at a time."

"That sounds good to me. You know where I'm at. I'm here for you any time you need me."

"Same here, Tee." He smiled and said, "I will see you when I get off the plane. " They hung up.

Rome felt 100% better. Trina has never let him down. She is the classic example of a good woman.

"Who needs Tamya when you got a T-bone steak at home?" Rome asked himself as the plane glided through the sky.

CHAPTER 8

Lately, Monica and Adonis were seeing each other more often. Adonis continued to teach Monica about her African history. The more Adonis taught her, the more amazed she was. Her biggest qualm was that she had not learned these important facts in school. Facts like, the first people to read and write were Black. They were the first people to have a system of higher learning. The first Physicians were Africans. The first Astrologers, Chemists, and Architects were Africans. The list goes on and on.

The more she learned the more pride she felt. At first, she couldn't swallow Adonis telling her that she was an African. "I'm not an African. I'm American. I wasn't born in Africa." Those were her first response.

"You're an African born in America. Just like all the other ethnic groups in America. For instance, take Italians. Their lineage goes back to Italy, thus the term Italian-American. Just because they weren't born in Italy doesn't change their true ethnicity."

It made perfect sense to Monica when Adonis broke it down to her. Adonis was good at breaking things all the way down; even a baby could understand his points.

Adonis told Monica the reason that Blacks in America deny their African heritage. "In slavery, Blacks were disconnected from their African culture and were told lies about Africans. They were told that Africans were savages, uncivilized, swinging from trees like monkeys with bones in their noses. Who would want to be associated with that type of image? That's why Blacks in America disassociate themselves from being African."

69

Although Adonis was seeing Monica frequently, Monica was still stripping. She was addicted to the lifestyle and the fast money. She did stop having sex for money. She came to terms with herself --on that part-- at least. Besides, she was making enough money just dancing. She never really liked that act of having sex with strangers. After the argument she had with Trina, Monica stopped selling her body.

Monica was becoming a household name in the stripping biz. Men packed the club to see her perform. She put on quite a spectacular performance.

She had her own personal introduction when she stripped. None of the other girls had a personal intro when they danced. Her intro started off with a hip hop beat playing. Then a man's voice would come on and ask, "Why do they call you Banana Pudding?

Then Monica's voice came on. "Because my skin is yellow like a Banana, and my pussy is creamy like pudding. Men go ape over Banana Pudding."

Then the man's voice would say, "Coming to the stage! The one! The only! Banana Pudding!"

Monica would make her entrance to the stage wearing a yellow patent leather cat-suit with yellow high heels. She was, by far, the sexiest, most attractive and voluptuous dancer in the club. She looked unreal, as if a cartoon artist drew the dimensions of her body; a flat stomach with a pierced belly button, perfect firm round breasts, thick thighs and a round ass with hips to match.

All the men were at her mercy. Money would be thrown from everywhere while she performed. The stage would be covered like a blanket of fresh snow. At the end of her show, she would have two grocery bags full of money.

To Monica, there was nothing like being a stripper. Monica got a rush every time she performed. She was a star when she was on stage. She received the same love as a famous actress or a pop star.

"I love Banana Pudding!" shouted one of her loyal fans as she exited the stage.

"I love you, too." Monica replied while blowing him a kiss.

The last couple of nights, Monica had been collecting in excess of $2,000 a night. Being a featured dancer got her more money. She was still getting offers for sex. One of her old costumers begged her one night to just spend one hour with him.

"I told you... I don't do that anymore." Monica couldn't understand some of these desperate men.

Monica loved the money. Letting go was going to be hard. She loved Adonis. What she loved most about Adonis was that he was into her mind and not just her body. Not once did Adonis make a comment or a gesture about sex. All of their time spent together was based on discussing knowledge.

Adonis didn't just speak on African history all the time. He asked Monica about her dreams and aspirations. He even asked her if she ever plan to have kids and raise a family. Adonis was the first man in Monica's life who didn't look at her like a piece of meat. To Adonis, Monica was a Black Queen, a Goddess. He treated her accordingly.

The things Adonis would say to Monica made her feel like she was royalty. One day Adonis told Monica something that touched the core of her being.

"They say that Cleopatra was one of the most beautiful women on earth. She was so beautiful that Julius Caesar was ready to denounce his thrown in Rome for her love. Shortly after he was murdered, his General, Mark Anthony, declared war with Rome when he fell in love with her. When I try to imagine how she might have looked, I think of you." Adonis spoke sincerely.

Monica was so flattered that she was at a loss for words. Out of impulse, she just hugged him tightly.

"That is the nicest thing that any man has ever said to me." As she hugged him, she silently shed tears. When she unlocked her embrace, Adonis had noticed the tears streaming down her face.

"Why are you crying? Is there something wrong?"

"No reason," Monica responded. "These are tears of joy, not tears of sorrow. I am so happy that I met someone like you, Adonis." She rubbed her hand on his cheeks.

"The feeling is mutual. The first time I laid eyes on you I knew that you were a very special lady."

"It's funny that you say that because the first time I saw you, something happened inside me that told me you were the one."

Adonis thought about their first meeting at the birthday party. He remembered her running to the bathroom. "What happened that day?"

"It was nothing wrong with you at all." She paused. "Maybe when we get old and have kids, I'll tell you." Adonis just left it at that.

It was conversations like this one that made Monica regret lying to Adonis about her being a stripper. She loved Adonis more than any man she has ever been with. It was a deep, real love because it was based on the mental connection and not only on physical attraction. If she was to lose Adonis because of her addiction to money, she would not be able to live with herself.

Monica wanted to know how Adonis felt about women who stripped for a living. She asked him some questions one day, pretending that the person she was referring to was not her.

"I have this friend who is a stripper. She met this guy who she really likes a lot. He doesn't know she's a stripper." She paused to see if he was suspicious. "So anyway, she asked me what she should do. Should she tell him or just keep it a secret? I want your opinion as a man."

She was doing well so far. Adonis didn't have a clue that she was really talking about herself. Adonis thought about her question for a minute before answering.

"In my opinion, women who strip in front of a crowd of men have no respect for themselves," Adonis said with conviction. Monica's heart fluttered. "And lying to him shows that she doesn't have any respect for him, either. So, if it was me, after she told me, or I found out, I'd probably want nothing to do with her. I think she should tell him if she really cares for him. Maybe he's the type of guy who likes the whole stripper thing. As for me I don't. I have a daughter to raise, and I wouldn't want my daughter to grow up and be a stripper. I don't condone it."

"OK, I'll take your advice to her and tell her what she should do. Thank you." Monica spoke nervously.

"Anytime, don't mention it." *Don't mention it* became their personal saying.

Monica was now caught between a rock and a hard place. Now she knew for sure where Adonis stood on the subject of strippers. If he knew that she was Banana Pudding, it would be curtains.

"What is more important? Stripping or Adonis?" she asked herself. "Adonis is definitely more important. I enjoy being Banana Pudding, but I enjoy being with Adonis more. If he only liked strippers, then everything would work out." These thoughts caused great conflict for Monica.

She had to reach a decision. It was going to be hard for her to stop stripping. She loved the attention she got from it. Nevertheless, Adonis made her feel ten times greater about herself as a Black Woman, a Queen.

He decided that she would strip for one more month, stack some paper and then quit. So that was it. Her mind was made up. She was going to quit the stripping business to be with Adonis. Monica thought about the way she spoke to Trina about stripping. She decided to give her a call to reconcile.

"Hello, Trina. How have you been?" Monica spoke humbly.

"I'm good, how about you?"

"I've been OK. Trina, I'm sorry for what I said to you. I felt really bad after our fight. You are right about what you said. Stripping is not what's really up."

Trina was shocked to hear her friend say these words. "I'm your big sister. I only want what's best for you, Monica. If I didn't care about you, I wouldn't even tell

74

you anything. You are a pretty and smart woman. You can be so much in life besides a stripper."

"Thank you for being there for me. You are the only family I have." Monica was getting misty eyed.

"Girl, you don't have to thank me. Anyway what's the latest with you and Adonis?"

"We have been seeing a lot of each other. He is so sweet to me. He is the main reason that I'm getting out of the stripper biz."

"I know you gave him some. Tell me all the details."

"That's what is so special about Adonis. He loves me for my mind and not my body. We haven't had sex yet. What we have is beyond the physical. Adonis makes love to *my mind.*"

"That is some deep shit. I'm happy for you. You deserve a good man." Trina paused before telling Monica her news. "Guess what?"

"Please don't make me guess."

"OK. Rome and I are back together. He bought me this expensive platinum chain with my name in diamonds."

"So you took him back?"

"No, not yet! We are just kicking it. Rome has changed. I think Adonis is rubbing off on him. They are always together. Rome doesn't even hang out anymore. He is always in the studio. He's teaching me African history also. He said Adonis is teaching him."

"That is good to hear. I always knew that Rome had a good side to him."

"Come over. Your nephew misses you, too."

"I'll be there in an hour." They both hung up.

Monica felt relieved now that they were on speaking terms again. She loved Trina like a sister. Her life would be incomplete without her sister. Now the only thing she had to fix was her occupation. After she took care of that, she felt that her life would be in order.

Rome's album was almost done. From the sounds of it, he had a hit album. The A&R Rep for Artist Records spoke to the big wigs about moving up Rome's release date. The response was that he could drop earlier if his single gained momentum.

Adonis advised Rome to do sixteen songs. Rome had eight hot songs that were finished. The more songs you have on your album, the more money you could get per unit sold. It made sense to Rome, even though he only wanted to do 12 songs.

The single that Rome wanted to put out first was a song dedicated to PT. Rome had gotten a tattoo on his right arm that read, "R.I.P. ANTWON 'PT' JOHNSON" with his birth date and death date. The song was a sentimental one dedicated to all the fallen soldiers in the struggle. Adonis thought it was a good choice as well.

Artist Records hesitated on Rome's first choice for the first single. The A&R rep talked them into it. It was a done deal. The first single would drop spring 2010. Before anything dropped, Rome had to complete a full length album. That meant a lot of time spent in the studio.

Recording an album was hard work, much harder than Rome anticipated. He spent 12 to 16 hours a day in the studio. He would eat, sleep, shower and shit in the studio. Rome practically lived in the studio. In the end, it would be worth it. He was living out his dreams.

"You think this part is hard? Wait till you go on promotional tour. Promotional means you don't get paid." Adonis tried to prepare Rome for things to come.

Rome was lucky to have a manager like Adonis, who schooled him on all the intricacies of the biz. Adonis was a seasoned vet in the music biz. He signed his first artist when he was 22, straight out of college. So he has experience under his belt. Adonis made sure that the label did everything they were supposed to do for his artists.

Adonis ensured that his artists were familiar with the "business" side of things as most artists focused on just the creative end of the industry. Adonis taught them about advertising and promotion budgets, credit lines, bonuses etc. Even though the artists had to recoup all of the money in the budget, they might as well take advantage of the perks. Only time would tell if Rome had what it took to be successful in the treacherous music industry.

CHAPTER 9

The investigation of PT and the young soldier's murder was spearheaded by homicide detectives Anthony Brown and Vincent Santiago. They knew two things so far. The detectives were sure that their mystery woman Cagney and her deceased sidekick, Lacey, were paid to do the hit. They also found out that the two vests and the guns used were registered to a homicide detective at the 88th precinct in Brooklyn. The vests were reported stolen from homicide detective Lisa Harris a year ago during a burglary.

Brown went to pay detective Harris a visit to inform her that her vest and one of her weapons were recovered. The other weapon was never found.

Detective Anthony Brown was a mulatto black man. He had curly hair and stood about 6'1. He had the lips and the high cheek bones of an African. He liked to describe himself as having the best of both worlds. Today, he was in the 88th to see Detective Harris and compare notes. She may have something on Cagney and Lacey.

"I'm Homicide Detective Brown from the 79th. I'm here to see Homicide Detective Lisa Harris," Brown said to the desk sergeant.

"This way, Detective Brown." A short, fat white man escorted him down a corridor.

There were about twenty desks in the large room with name plates on each. Now he had to find the one with Detective Harris' name on it. He looked to his right, then to his left and there she was. It didn't take long to notice Detective Harris. Not only was she the only woman, but she was fine. Brown grabbed his tie and tightened it at the neck to make sure he looked his best. He walked over to her desk nice and smooth. She was on the phone and pretended to ignore him when he stood in front of her desk.

"Yes, we know your husband was killed, but we don't have any leads. As soon as we know something, you will," Detective Harris said to a distressed widow. She looked at Detective Brown in his eyes while he was waiting. "OK, Mrs. Gonzales, we're working on it. Bye." She looked at Detective Brown. "Can I help you sir?"

"Yes." Brown flashed his badge. "I'm Homicide Detective Brown from the 79th. I want to inform you that your vest and one of your weapons were recovered at a murder scene on Gates Ave."

"I know that. I already got my property back. The vest was all shot up. What else can I help you with?"

"Well, one of the suspects was admitted to KCH on the day of the shooting. The officer thought she was an innocent bystander. My partner and I have reasons to believe that she is one half of the infamous female hit team Cagney and Lacey."

"I heard about them, but I'm not sure if they are real. They are more legend than reality. No one seems to know what they look like. Down here at the 88th, we are starting to think they are just a legend, a myth."

"We believed the same until something lead us to believe otherwise. On the day of the shooting, we noticed that one of the females who was shot up by the officers in the bodega had on a wig. When we called KCH, the nurse told us that the so-called innocent bystander had on one, too."

"So what does that mean?"

"Five years ago, an old lady was looking out of her window when she heard gunshots. Shortly after, she witnessed two Black women running out of the building with two suitcases. All she could tell about their identity was that they wore wigs. So the wigs are like their MO so to speak."

"I see. That is interesting because we had a description like that also at a homicide we were investigating a year ago." Harris paused to think. "What happened to the living culprit who was in KCH?"

"She slipped our grasp and disappeared. We know that there is only one left now. That one is probably Cagney."

"How could you assume that? She could be Lacey."

"Well, considering that the deceased real name was Stacey, we figured she was Lacey."

"That's what I call good detective work," Harris said with an admiring smile.

Detective Brown wrote his number on a card and handed it to Detective Harris. "If you find any leads, please call me. Or, if you just want to have dinner with me tonight, that will be nice too."

"My, my, aren't we straight to the point. I like that in a man. I just might take you up on your offer."

"Eight o'clock sounds good to you?"

"Perfect. I'll see you at eight."

Brown left the 88th feeling good that he had visited Harris. There was something about a woman with a badge that he couldn't resist. He was looking forward to the date. He needed to unwind anyway. Homicide work can get stressful.

Brown's work was not done yet. He had to find out who ordered the hit, and why. Narcotics identified PT as a drug dealer. He had a prior drug arrest on the same block. The hit was most likely over drug territory, Brown thought. As he thought, his cell phone rang. "Detective Brown," he answered.

"I just found out a bit of information on the Gates Ave murders. It seems that PT had a partner named Jerome Chandler a/k/a/ Rome. And check this out, our buddy Rome, is supposed to be a hot rapper," Detective Santiago reported.

"Do you have any idea about the whereabouts of our supposedly hot rapper so we can take him in for questioning?"

"I've got an address on Gates but I went there and he doesn't live there anymore. No other address has been confirmed."

"Well, at least we have some leads. I just finished meeting with Detective Harris from the 88th. She also has reports on two wigged Black Women. She is going to be working with us."

"I'll meet you at the precinct in an hour."

Detective Brown wanted Cagney badly. He vowed to keep on her trail until he caught her. He was intrigued by this female killer, especially one who was able to elude him for this long. As far as Brown was concerned, Cagney's time was up. He would put his career on it. He always gets his man, or in this case, his woman.

Monica and Adonis' daughter, Makeda, became very close.

"Daddy, where is Monica? I want to see Monica she is so pretty," Makeda would ask her father every day.

"I know baby. She is at home. Let's give her a call and see if she wants to hang out with us."

Monica never turned down the chance to be with Makeda. Not only because she loved Adonis, but because Makeda needed a maternal figure. She reminded Monica of herself when she was a little girl. Makeda never ceased to amaze Monica with the things she would say. It was like talking to an adult.

"You like my Daddy, don't you Monica?"

"Yes, I do. Why do you ask?"

"I can tell. He likes you, too."

"How do you know?"

"I always hear him talking about you. Monica this and Monica that."

"Oh really!"

"Mm-Hmm, you would think you two were married."

That comment coming from a 5-year old girl shocked Monica. What does a five year old know about marriage? Monica thought. Nowadays these kids know more than you think.

"Can you do my hair like yours, Monica? I want to look pretty like you."

"You are already pretty; more than me."

"When I grow up, I want to be a model just like you."

Monica became nervous when Makeda made that statement.

"How did you know I was a model?" Monica spoke in a worried tone.

"I heard my Daddy telling Grandma about you on the phone. He said you were a model, and that you are intelligent and pretty."

"Oh I see." Things are getting a little deep. Adonis is telling his mother about me. That means he has developed some real feelings. These thoughts lead to mixed emotions for Monica.

Monica was glad to know that Adonis was telling his mother about her. However, she wasn't too happy about lying to him about what she does for a living.

She thought if she could get through this month stripping without Adonis finding out, it would soon be over for Banana Pudding. Her stripping days would be a rap. Not tonight though, she was scheduled to work, so Banana Pudding lived on...

One of Rome's homeboys just got released from doing five years in prison. His name was Marty, but in the hood he was known as Rambo. He got that name for shooting automatic weapons at his enemies.

Rambo had put on quite a few pounds while he sat in jail. He went from 160 pounds soaking wet, to 225 pounds of solid muscle. His waves were spinning, pearly whites grinning.

Rambo was trying to get his freak on. What better place to go and see half naked beautiful women than at the strip club. Looking at all those porno magazines in jail will make a brother stay up in a strip club.

A lot has changed since Rambo left the hood. None of the homies were around when Rambo came home but

Rome. The rest of the fellows were either dead or doing long prison terms.

Rambo heard about PT's murder, but he didn't know all of the details. All he knew was that two gun-toting females did the shooting. He asked Rome questions about the PT's murder.

"Man, shit was crazy. We were standing by my truck when these two chicks came walking our way. I didn't pay them any mind. I didn't see any guns at first. One of the workers went to serve them. He saw the guns and yelled out for us to get down. I looked at the chicks and then they were shooting! I hit the ground and rolled under the truck. PT pulled out the 9 millimeter and emptied the whole clip. He hit one in the chest three times. The other one hit PT in the neck and head. I knew he was gone."

"That's fucked up. I heard big, bitch ass Walt had something to do with it."

"Yeah, we had a run-in with him like a month before the shit happened. PT put the 9 mill to Walt's head because he came around here stunting. He said we couldn't get money on Gates."

"So what's up? Let's ride on his punk ass."

"Right now I'm taking it easy. My album is about to drop, and the last thing I need is to catch a case. Plus homicide is hot. You just came home. You don't need that kind of drama. I got a spot for you on tour with me if you with it."

"I heard you were hitting that R&B chick, Tamya."

"Fuck that bitch. She played herself. She was fucking with that bitch ass R&B faggot, Authentic. I knocked son out in St. Louis."

"Word! That's what's up. What's good with some pussy? You know a brother trying to get his freak on."

"I got you, son. There is this exclusive strip club in Mount Vernon called Sue's Rendezvous. I haven't been there, but I heard about some chick named Banana Pudding who strips there. She is supposed to be the baddest chick there."

"Let's go. I'm ready to see some ass shaking. A brother's been away from ass for five years."

They got in Rome's Escalade and drove to Sue's. While they drove, Rome played music from his forthcoming album. He liked to see the reaction of the listener. After all, the listeners are the ones who can make you or break you.

Rambo was nodding his head out of control. "Yo, son, your shit is off the hook. I'm feeling this shit."

"Thanks, son. I got this song that I dedicated to PT. It's going to be my first single." Rome skipped the disc to the song.

A mellow sound mixed with a strong beat and serious lyrics changed their mood. They were quiet for the rest of the ride. Both of them were deep in thought.

When they arrived at Sue's Rendezvous, they couldn't believe how packed it was. There were gorgeous women of every size and flavor walking around in thongs, mingling with men.

"Yo son, this shit is crazy," Rambo said like a kid in a candy store.

"I know. I never been here but it is the best one I've seen."

As Rome spoke, two voluptuous women strolled up to them and began rubbing their asses on them.

"Would you like a lap dance?" One of the women asked Rambo.

He looked at her like he was going to eat her.

"No doubt. Rome you got me?"

"No question." Rome peeled off about $200 in singles. Rambo and the stripper went to a VIP to handle their business. Rome declined the offer from the other woman.

All of a sudden the lights went dim and a thumping beat sounded over the speakers. Then a man's voice came over the beat.

"Why do they call you Banana Pudding?"

"Because I'm yellow like a banana, and my pussy is creamy like pudding. Men go ape over Banana Pudding."

"Coming to the stage, the one, the only, Banana Pudding!"

All the men rushed the stage. Rome wanted to see exactly why everyone was raving over this woman. He got a little closer to the stage. Out came a beautiful goddess wearing a yellow patent-leather halter top and skin-tight patent leather pants. She had on thigh high patent-leather hooker boots.

Monica began her show by shaking her ass and holding her breast. Then she would slowly take off her top and then slowly strip down to her thong.

"Damn, she looks a lot like Monica. No, Banana Pudding can't be Monica," Rome whispered himself.

As Rome focused on her a little better, he couldn't believe his eyes. It was Monica. "Monica is Banana Pudding. This can't be." Rome said out loud to himself in disbelief.

He went closer to the stage and it was confirmed. Monica is Banana Pudding. He knew she had a body, but he has never seen her like this. She was the talk of the town.

What is Adonis going to think when he finds out that his girl is a stripper named Banana Pudding? I know how he feels about strippers because I asked him to come with us, Rome thought.

"I think women who strip are the lowest women on earth. Go ahead and have fun. I'm not into that." That was Adonis's response when Rome asked him to come to Sue's with him tonight.

Good thing he didn't come, Rome thought.

All this time Monica had Adonis, even Rome, thinking that she was a model at Fresh Faces. It was easy to believe her because she was pretty enough to be a model.

She continued her show. Rome saw why she was the star of the show. She was good at what she does. Any man on earth would enjoy watching her strip.

When she was finished with her routine, she exited the stage. As usual, her fans began shouting, "WE WANT BANANA PUDDING!" It was like a war chant.

She came back out on stage bowing and blowing kisses to her fans. That's when she spotted Rome in the crowd. The expression on her face went from appreciation to shame. She ran off the stage trying to cover what little of her body she could.

Monica was so ashamed that Rome saw her strip and now her cover was blown. Rome was like a brother to her. She was disgusted with herself. What really affected her was the thought that Rome would tell Adonis. She couldn't allow him to do that. Monica had to go out there and tell Rome to keep this a secret. She knew he was going to tell Adonis. They were like best friends. She couldn't afford that happening.

She quickly got dressed and went out into the crowd to find Rome. Men everywhere were making lewd noises and gawking at her.

"Hey Banana Pudding, let me put my dick in your creamy pudding and stir it up," one guy said as she walked pass.

Rome saw her coming his way. He couldn't even look her in the eyes. He would never see her in the same way again.

"Rome, we need to talk." Monica spoke like it was a matter of life and death.

"Go ahead, talk *Banana Pudding*," Rome said sarcastically.

"I'm serious Rome. Please don't tell Adonis. I love him so much. Tonight is the last night I'm stripping. I promise. Just don't tell him. "

Rome heard the sincerity in her voice and thought about Monica's plea.

"I won't, but you have to stop tonight. If I hear that you're still doing it, I'm telling him."

"Thank you, Rome. You don't have to worry. I'm finished with this shit."

Monica walked back through the crowd and approached the owner of Sue's Rendezvous. She told him that she was leaving the game. He tried to get her to reconsider, but she insisted that tonight was the last night for Banana Pudding.

88

When Monica exited through the back, she stopped by the trash dumpster and threw away all of her stripping costumes.

"That's it, no more Banana Pudding. Banana Pudding is dead." She got into her BMW 645 and drove off, never to return to Sue's.

CHAPTER 10

Rome heard that homicide Detectives Brown and Santiago were looking for him for questioning. Adonis advised him to go down to the precinct to answer the questions with a lawyer present.

"Did you tell anyone?" Adonis asked Rome.

"Hell no!"

"Well you have nothing to worry about."

Rome and Adonis went to the 79th precinct with attorney Peter Stokaski. When they got there, Stokaski reminded Rome what to say. "Remember what I told you. You don't know anything. You know the deceased from high school and that's it. Got it?"

"Yeah I got it."

They entered the 79th precinct and approached the desk sergeant. "I'm Attorney Peter Stokaski. I'm here to see Detectives Brown and Santiago for a questioning of my client, Mr. Jerome Chandler. It has come to our attention that they have been looking for my client in connection with the Gates Ave murder. So here we are."

"Wait right here a second." The desk sergeant picked up the phone and informed Brown that he had visitors. He briefly told him what the lawyer said the visit was about. The sergeant escorted them to a room with a table and three chairs "Have a seat and someone will be with you shortly."

Two minutes later, Brown strolled into the room.

"Mr. Chandler or should I call you Rome?" Brown said in a cynical manner.

"Rome is OK."

There was a small tape recorder on the table. Brown activated the recorder and began his line of questioning. "Mr. Chandler, I mean, Rome. Where were you on September 6th at approximately 3:30pm?"

"I was with my manager, Adonis Nkosi," Rome nodded towards Adonis.

"You were not on Gates Ave between Marcus Garvey and Troop with Antwon PT Johnson?"

"No, I was not."

"Are you sure? We have reasons to believe that you were on Gates at that time."

Peter interjected, "I object to your line of questioning. My client has already stated where he was on the said day."

Detective Brown took a deep breath. "OK, where do you know PT from?"

"I know him from high school. We were friends."

"Word on the streets is that you and PT were partners, and have a drug business on Gates Ave. Is that true?"

"No. I am a professional recording artist signed to Artist Records."

Stokaski shook his head in approval of Rome's answer.

"According to our arrest records, it is possible that you were selling drugs on Gates Ave before." Brown paused to see Rome's reaction. His face was stone. "Anyway, do you know a Mr. Walter Green from Quincy Ave.?"

"Yes, I know him."

"Were you and Walter friends or enemies?"

"We were not the best of friends, but we weren't enemies either."

"Is it possible that you and Walter had beef over drug territory that you and PT controlled?"

"No, because me and PT, didn't control any drug territory. I told you before, I don't sell drugs."

Brown knew that this was going nowhere.

If this cock sucking lawyer wasn't here I could put some pressure on this prick and squeeze the truth out of him, Brown thought to himself.

Brown knew as long as the lawyer was present, he was asking for trouble if he broke the rules. "That's all for now, but if I were you, I would stick to rapping and leave the streets alone."

They left the precinct. Rome felt relief now that it was over. With that out of the way, now he could focus on his music.

"You did good Rome. You shouldn't hear from them anymore. If you do, you have my number." Stokaski drove off in his CL 600 Benz.

"That wasn't so bad, was it?" Adonis said to Rome. "Now let's go get our Queens and go celebrate."

Trina and Monica were with Makeda and Tavon at a local park. The kids were playing on the swings and monkey bars. Monica and Trina sat on a bench talking.

"Girl, I was so embarrassed when I looked into the crowd and saw Rome. " Monica winced at the thought. "I ran backstage, put my clothes on, came out, and begged Rome not to tell Adonis."

"I know...Rome called and told me. He said, 'Tee, did you know Monica was Banana Pudding?' I wanted to bust out laughing because of the way he said it."

"You should have seen the look on his face when he saw me," Monica paused. "Well, Banana Pudding is behind me now. Anything that I'm ashamed to do in front of my brother, I don't need to be doing." She spoke with conviction.

"I hear that girl. What are you going to do now?"

"I have an appointment with Fresh Faces on Monday morning. I've always wanted to be a model. You know how I like new clothes. Plus, all my life people have always told me that I could be a model."

"Good luck! I hope they hire you. They should."

Adonis and Rome pulled up in Adonis' midnight blue Range Rover. He and Rome got out and walked towards the girls. After both couples exchanged pleasantries, they sat to discuss the meeting.

"How did it go at the precinct?" Trina asked.

"It went real smooth. They won't be fucking with me anymore."

"Good, because you don't need the bullshit right now."

"Let's all go to dinner. Get the kids and let's celebrate," Adonis said.

Everyone got into the Range Rover and went to a nice restaurant on City Island. Monica and Adonis had become closer. Monica had more time to spend with him since she stopped stripping. She felt more at ease now that she didn't have to lie about her occupation. Monica concentrated on developing a serious relationship with her King.

They spent every day together. Although sex had not occurred, there were moments when things got hot. The sexual half of their relationship was bound to happen. Monica wanted Adonis more than she has ever wanted any man in her life. It was only a matter of time before Adonis either made a move on her sexually, or she was going to rape him.

Adonis was still mourning the death of Tammy. Monica knew that Adonis had not made love to a woman since the death of his wife. For that reason, she was patient about them having sex. However, soon she felt like she would explode if he didn't make love to her.

While they ate, Adonis couldn't help staring at Monica. She looked more radiant than ever. He couldn't put a finger on what it was, but he noticed that she was more into him lately. For the past week or so, she has made herself very available to him. They ate lunch every day, and she even spent the night at Adonis' brownstone on a couple occasions.

Maybe it's time to deal with the physical. It has been six months now. Tonight is the night, Adonis thought to himself.

Monica aroused Adonis so much that while he ate his food, he looked at her, fantasizing that it was her on a platter.

Monica couldn't help but notice the sexy way Adonis looked at her. She felt the heat of his stare all the way down to her crotch. She always seemed to get moist thinking about making love to Adonis. Tonight, the physical attraction was so intense you could cut it with a knife. Monica blushed as Adonis stared at her while sucking on a crab leg. She was feeling so hot that she had

94

to unbutton a few buttons on her Prada blouse. Her vagina was tingling so much that if she accidentally rubbed it, she might climax.

It was definitely time for the second phase of their relationship. It was inevitable that sex would occur between two consenting adults who were in love. What made this experience so great was the fact that they spent most of their time getting to know each other mentally. That would make the sex that much better.

When the meal was finished, Adonis asked Trina if Makeda could spend the night with her. Trina agreed to keep her for the night.

They dropped Rome, Trina, and the kids off at Trina's house. Rome knew something was about to go down between Adonis and Monica. He noticed the stares that they stole at each other during dinner. Rome knew Adonis' situation about his wife and how he had not been with a woman in a year.

"Take it easy tiger," Rome playfully whispered in Adonis' ear.

The drive to Adonis' brownstone was an awkward one. Neither one spoke for half the ride. They both just stole glances at one another. Both were feeling the heat of the moment. They both knew what was about to go down. There was no fronting involved. It was time to get it popping.

Adonis stopped at a light. As he waited for the light to turn green, he looked at his Queen. Monica looked back at him, and for that second, they were locked in each other's stare. Monica couldn't take it anymore. She reached the top half of her body over to the driver's side and she passionately kissed Adonis on the mouth. Adonis responded by grabbing her, almost pulling her out of her seat. They locked lips like two double doors. They were so engrossed in the kiss that they didn't notice the light turned green. Cars were beeping their horns trying to get them to move.

Adonis pressed the gas. He couldn't wait to get her to his brownstone. When they finally reached the brownstone, Adonis had to take a deep breath to get his composure. As soon as they stepped in the door of the apartment, Monica pushed Adonis up against a wall, pressed her body against his, and kissed him ferociously. She was the aggressive one, attacking him like a lioness.

Then Adonis' male dominance kicked in. He picked her up off the floor, tossed her onto the couch, and pounced on her like prey. She unbuttoned her blouse. He grabbed her perfect breasts. He sucked on them as if he was famished. It drove Monica wild.

She unbuttoned his pants and reached for his manhood. What she felt made her even hornier. Adonis was blessed with a penis that could satisfy any woman. She took off her pants, and stood before him in her thong and bra. Adonis stripped down to his boxers.

Adonis slowed down the pace by caressing her whole body. He explored her body as if it was a planet. He rubbed and kissed every curve, and sucked her toes. Adonis passionately rubbed her hair and palmed her face in his hands. He made sure that he was gentle with her because he wanted to make love to her. He didn't want to "fuck" her.

Adonis picked her up in his arms and carried her up the stairs to his room. Monica held on to his strong arms. She had to keep taking deep breaths to keep from losing control. She wanted to sexually attack him, but she also wanted to make love. It would be something different for her, considering that she only had sex with her costumers.

This feels so right. Oh God, thank you for bringing this man into my life. I love this man.

They spoke without using words. They were so in tune with each other mentally that every touch brought on new pleasure. Never before did Monica feel what she was feeling that night. It was like they were one. Their hearts were in sync and their breathing seemed like it flowed together. They formed a perfect union.

This woman is so beautiful. I'm so glad that my spirit guided me to her. I know it was meant for us to be together. I love this woman.

After an hour of kissing and caressing, Adonis carefully placed his penis to the opening of her vagina. He gently put it in. There was a deep sigh of relief that came from both of them. He went deeper and deeper with each stroke. Monica made sounds of pure pleasure.

Adonis felt his loins swelling up ready to release. He wanted to hold it, but he couldn't. It had been so long since he had any sex that he was ready to ejaculate. It was OK with Monica because she already climaxed twice.

"Baby, I'm coming! " He tried to pull his penis out.

"No! Leave it in. Please cum in me. I want to have your baby."

Those words pushed Adonis over the edge. He couldn't control himself. His hips began to buck. His knees started to buckle and his eyes were rolling into the back of his head. He released his sperm in her with the hopes of making a baby. They both had thoughts of creating a new life; a baby made out of love.

After he ejaculated into her, he lay there inside of her, passionately kissing her all over her face. He was feeling the euphoria from a year of abstinence, coupled with true love. He was on a natural high.

Monica was also feeling the effects of true love's energy. This was the first time in her life that she felt complete with a man. Her soul was screaming out inside of her because this was real love.

It was now complete. Both the mental and the physical realms were joined. Their relationship had been purely mental up until this point. Now they both understood each other on a spiritual plane.

The beauty of their relationship was that they spent time getting to know each other mentally before having sex. Adonis made love to her mind, and then he made love to her body. That is the correct order. Adonis knew how perfect relationships were formed. He understood that sex can be a spiritual experience if you make the mental connection first. So many relationships fail because they go straight to the sex instead of first entertaining the mind. When you know your mate's mind, then the sex becomes a more intense and spiritual experience.

"Adonis," Monica whispered his name.

"Yes, my Queen."

"I love you." She gave him the most sincere look she ever gave anyone.

"I love you more." He gave her his most charming smile. She smiled back. "Where do we go from here? I mean, what are we?"

"You are my soul mate, Monica. I knew that from the first time I laid eyes on you. I felt something when I touched your hand the first time. The last time I felt like this was when I met my wife, Tammy."

"I know exactly what you felt because that's what I felt when I first saw you. And when you touched me, something happened that never happened to me before. That's why I ran to the bathroom that day. I didn't understand what was happening to me, but now I understand."

"I understand, too. This is true, real love. It was love at first sight."

Adonis held her tightly. She fit perfectly in his arms. They held each other like this until they both fell soundly asleep.

The next day they both woke up feeling like new and different people, knowing that they had finally crossed that barrier into physical sex. There was a sense of oneness with each other now. There was no more holding back. They both felt an enormous feeling of serenity.

Adonis had an idea. He wanted to take Monica to Long Island to meet his parents. "You have anything to do today?"

"No. I just want to be with you."

"Let's go get Makeda and go out to Long Island to visit my parents."

Monica got quiet. She was nervous about meeting his parents.

"First take me home so I can get dressed."

Adonis dropped Monica off at her apartment. "I love you, Adonis," Monica said before kissing him.

"I love you, too. I'll be back for you at 12 o'clock on the dot."

Monica was on cloud nine. She never thought she would find a love like this. She walked around her condo with a permanent grin pasted to her face. Everything reminded her of Adonis. She couldn't wait for him to return.

Adonis was back at Monica's condo at 11:55 sharp. Monica was ready. She felt nervous about meeting his parents.

What if they don't like me? I will just be myself, Monica thought to herself.

"I like going to Grandma's house," Makeda said. "You're going to like Grandma's house, too. It's nice you'll see." Monica didn't respond; she was too nervous to talk. Adonis noticed her nervousness.

"Don't worry, honey. I know you're nervous, but trust me, they will like you." Adonis was trying to ease her mind.

The drive from Brooklyn to Central Islip, Long Island, took 45 minutes. Central Islip is literally the center of Long Island. It was the suburbs, very different from Brooklyn. It wasn't far from the city, so you could get the best of both worlds.

Adonis grew up in Central Islip. His parents owned the same house all of his life. Adonis was the oldest of three siblings. His sister, Chareese, was two years younger than him. He had a little brother named Geno who was seven years younger. His sister lived in New Orleans. His little brother lived with his parents.

When they entered the driveway, Monica noticed the manicured lawn. It was a nice, big house. Monica imagined what it would be like growing up in a house like this.

Adonis' mother was waiting at the door when they got out of the truck. Monica took one look at her and immediately knew where Adonis got his good looks from. She was a beautiful woman. Evidence of aging showed on her face. Nevertheless, she aged gracefully.

"Hi, baby." Mrs. Nkosi said to her son, kissing him on his right cheek. "Where is my grand baby? Come here and give Grandma a kiss."

"Hi, Grandma." Makeda said as she hugged and kissed her Grandmother.

"And who is this pretty young woman? You must be Monica. Son, you sure do know how to pick them. It is nice to finally meet you, Monica. Adonis speaks highly of you."

The warm reception that Mrs. Nkosi gave her put Monica at ease.

"It is nice to meet you, too, Mrs. Nkosi." Monica smiled.

When Adonis and Monica entered the house, Adonis' father was in the living room watching a basketball game. He got out of his chair to greet them. He was tall with broad shoulders, like his son. His complexion was darker than Adonis' and Adonis' mother. Monica could tell that Mr. Nkosi was as handsome as his son in his day.

"What's up dad? How're you doing?"

"I'm doing all right, son. How about you?"

"I'm fair for a square. Dad, this is Monica."

Mr. Nkosi extended his hand and shook Monica's hand. "How are you doing, Monica? It's nice to meet you."

"Nice to meet you, too, Mr. Nkosi."

"It's about time you brought yourself home, son. I haven't seen you in almost a year."

"I've been very busy lately. But I plan on visiting more often."

Adonis sat down with his father to watch the game. Basketball was Adonis' dream before he got involved in the music biz. He would have made it to the NBA if music didn't catch his eye.

"Come on in here, Monica, and help me in the kitchen."

Monica went into the kitchen with Mrs. Nkosi. Mrs. Nkosi was a gourmet cook. She was cooking some collard greens, baked macaroni and cheese, sweet potatoes and beef roast. The aroma smelled delicious.

"So, Adonis tells me that you're a model."

"Yes, but I haven't been getting much work lately."

"A pretty girl like you should stay with work in that field."

That compliment made Monica blush.

"You know you are the first woman my son has dated since his wife passed away last year. You must be very special to him."

"I feel very special when I'm with Adonis. Your son is the most intelligent and sweetest man I've ever met."

"Yeah, Adonis is something. I love my Adonis." Mrs. Nkosi got out of her chair. "Hold on a minute Monica. I'm going to show you something!" Mrs. Nkosi said with excitement.

She went upstairs and came back with a stack of photo albums. She put the stack of photo albums on the table. "I'm going to start when he was a baby."

She opened the first book and pointed to a picture of a baby boy sitting on a rug holding a teddy bear.

"Oh, look at him. He was a pretty baby. He is so cute." Monica spoke in that feminine tone that woman always use when they look at baby pictures.

Mrs. Nkosi flipped through a few more pictures of Adonis as a toddler, then she got to the pictures of him in kindergarten. "When Adonis was a baby, his nickname was Dukey, because he use to do-do all the time."

Monica found his childhood nickname hilarious. They went through the entire stack of photo albums. Monica was enjoying herself.

Mrs. Nkosi was very down to earth. Adonis was a lot like his Mother.

"Hey Dukey ! Come here for a minute," Monica said jokingly.

"Come on Mom. Why did you have to tell her that name?"

"Oh boy, everybody had a nickname when they were babies," Mrs. Nkosi said in her defense. "Come on Monica, let's set the table. Adonis, go tell your father that dinner is ready."

The food smelled and looked delicious. Everyone took their place at the table. After everyone made their plates, Mr. Nkosi began blessing the food. "God please bless this food we are about to receive for the strength of our bodies and the nourishment of our souls." He was interrupted by the opening of the front door. It was Adonis's little brother, Geno.

Geno walked into the kitchen and just stood there looking at everyone with a confused look on his face. Geno was a slim, shorter, younger version of Adonis. As he stood there in a daze, it became obvious why he was in such a stupor; he was high.   He reeked of marijuana smoke.

Mr. Nkosi finished saying the grace as if Geno was not even there.   After he was done with the grace, Mrs. Nkosi took that time to scold her baby boy. "What is wrong with you coming in here smelling like a ton of marijuana? Adonis, you better talk to your brother before I kill him."

"What's up big bro? Who is the broad?" He paused and then answered his own question. "Oh, that must be your new girl- right, right." He spoke with a silly smirk on his face.

Adonis didn't even answer his little brother. He just looked at him and continued eating.

Geno was a product of too much spoiling. He was the baby, so he got everything that he wanted. He didn't do anything all day but smoke weed. If it wasn't for his parents, he would be homeless.

"Geno, I have to talk to you after I eat." Adonis spoke with seriousness in his tone.

Mr. Nkosi acted like nothing was going on. He just sat and ate his food. Geno came and went as he pleased, and Mr. Nkosi paid him no mind. Mr. Nkosi thought it was best that he did it that way as he felt like killing Geno. That's how mad Geno made his father. Geno was the reason why Mr. Nkosi had high blood pressure. So instead of killing him or dying from high blood pressure, he left Geno alone.

Mrs. Nkosi was the only one who said anything to Geno.   However, she wasn't stern enough. She would scold him and then give him money an hour later. Geno never took her seriously.

"That's what I'm talking about," Geno said, rubbing his hand together. "Some eats...A brother hungrier than a mother..." Geno stopped himself before he cursed in the house.

"Oh, no you don't! Go wash your hands before you go putting them in my pots."

They made small talk over dinner. They spoke about everything; sports, fashion, politics. When everyone finished eating, Adonis took the time to talk to Geno outside.

"Listen Geno, you're twenty-three years old now. It's time to grow up. You're not a little kid anymore. It would be an excuse if you were still eighteen. How would you like to move to Brooklyn with me and work for my company as a co-manager?" There was a moment of silence. "The pay is good, but you can't get high during work hours."

After some thought, Geno said. "No doubt, I can do that. When can I start?"

"Rome's single is dropping this spring. That's when you can start. After you get some money, you can move out and get your own spot."

"You got yourself a co-manager."

"Remember, no smoking during working hours. That's from 8 am to 5 pm."

"It's supposed to be from 9 to 5."

"One hour is for lunch."

They went back inside. Everyone was gathered in the living room conversing. Adonis looked at his watch and noticed it was getting late. He had to drive back to

Brooklyn. Everyone said their farewells. Monica and Makeda got into the Range while Adonis finished up his talk with Geno.

"Don't forget what I said. I'm going to help you, but not if you don't help yourself."

"I got you."

"I love you, Geno. I want to see you do well."

Adonis gave Geno a goodbye hug, jumped in the Range and then drove off.

"I had a very nice time today with your family. You have a beautiful family. Thank you for bringing me to meet your parents."

"Don't mention it," said Adonis with a warm smile.

Monica thought about what her life would have been like if she would have grown up with a family like Adonis'. She thought about how hard it was growing up in the ghetto with two drug addicts for parents.

Monica had various thoughts running through her mind during the drive back to Brooklyn: I would probably be a doctor or a lawyer. I would not have been a stripper. I know my life would have been a lot easier. Guess it was meant for me to grow up like I did. I will make sure that my kids don't ever have to go through what I did. And that's a promise.

CHAPTER 11

Today was a very important day for Monica. She had an appointment to meet with the head agent at Fresh Faces. They were the biggest modeling agency in the world. Monica had a professional portfolio that she had done in the beginning of the year. The pictures were tastefully done. Everyone thought the pictures would win her a modeling job. She never took the idea seriously until now.

Monica was looking spectacular in her Armani business woman suit. She was shining like a diamond. The three-inch heels make her look 6'1 even. Without heels, she was normally 5'10. That was considered tall for a woman. With the heels on, she was an Amazon. Her appointment was for 10:00 am. She arrived five minutes early, a habit she acquired from Adonis.

"Hi, I'm Monica Pernell. I have an appointment with Mrs. Thackston."

The receptionist looked at Monica and then at her list. "Yes, I see your name here, Mrs. Pernell. Have a seat and someone will be right with you." The receptionist spoke into the intercom, "Mrs. Thackston, your 10 o'clock appointment is here."

"Send her in."

"You may go in now. Good luck."

"Thank you."

When she entered the office, Mrs. Thackston was on the phone. Monica stood until Mrs. Thackston was finished to offer her a seat. While Monica was standing, Mrs. Thackston noticed how tall she was. She could not see that Monica was wearing three-inch heels because of the desk.

"How are you doing today, Ms. Pernell?" Mrs. Thackston extended her hand. Monica nervously shook her hand.

"I'm fine, Mrs. Thackston, how about yourself?"

"I'm fine, please call me Pamela. Mrs. Thackston sounds too much like a principal. Please have a seat."

Pamela had the look of a professional businesswoman. She had blonde hair and blue eyes that sat behind expensive wire rimmed frames. She had the features of the average white model seen in the magazines.

"I see here that you have no formal training or experience in modeling. From the looks of your portfolio, you pose like a professional. You're one of the natural photogenic types."

"All my life people have been telling me that I could be a model because of my height."

"You can definitely be a model. The only problem is that we require experience. We don't have the time to train you."

Monica's heart almost sank to her stomach. "I see. But wouldn't it be experience enough if I did some work. I mean nobody really has experience until they're hired, right?" Monica sounded desperate.

"Not necessarily. Most of our models have been groomed since they were little girls. Runway work and photos are not as easy as it looks." Pamela paused and stared at Monica. She took off her glasses and turned her head to the side. "I know what I can use you for. Recently there has been a lot of request from our agency for ethnic models to appear in rap videos. A lot of our Black and Latino models have been getting loads of work doing rap videos. We get so many requests that we don't have enough variety for the directors to choose from. That's why you see the same models in the videos."

Monica thought about what Pamela was saying. Most of the rap videos that she saw were just like the strip club; half naked women walking around shaking their ass. "I think I can do that."

"Great. You have yourself a job. Welcome aboard Fresh Faces International."

Monica had a feeling of extreme joy. Even though she would be doing just rap videos, she thought about the opportunity to move up to bigger things. Posing in front of a camera half-naked was the same as being half naked in a strip club. Now the feeling of guilt about lying was gone. Now she was officially an employee of Fresh Faces.

"It's spring again," Rome sang, imitating the hit song by Biz Markie. This spring could change Rome's life forever. His first single was about to hit the stores.

Rome and Adonis was at Artist Records headquarters in downtown Manhattan. They had a meeting with the director of A&R department named Fat Tommy. Fat Tommy was not fat at all and as a matter of fact, he was skinny and short. He had a lot of clout at Artist Records.

"The response your single is getting is phenomenal. People everywhere are requesting it. Now, let's see if all these people go out to buy the album tomorrow."

Tomorrow was Tuesday March 30th. All the stores across the country had Rome's "FALLEN SOLDIERS" album on their shelves. Artist Records shipped 200,000 units. Technically, Rome has sold 200,000 units to the retail stores. When those 200,000 units are sold to the customers, then Artist Records will be pleased with Rome. From the response of the people, his sales should sky-rocket. Only time would tell.

Rome couldn't sleep that night. He and Trina were back together now and he was happy to be living with her and his son, Tavon. However, he was tossing and turning all night long as he thought about his album.

"Baby, come on. Lie down and get some sleep," Trina said as she was concerned about Rome's insomnia.

"I can't sleep. I tried, but thinking about how many records I got to sell got my mind twisted. If I don't sell, not only will I get dropped from the label, I won't get signed again."

"Don't worry. I know you are going to sell records. Your single was number one on the hot eight at eight. People are going to be lined up at the stores waiting to buy your album." As she spoke, she rubbed his back.

"Let's hope so. This is my only way out of the hood." He closed his eyes and he eventually fell asleep.

The next day when Rome awoke, he and Adonis took a ride around NYC to all the major record stores. People were lined up, but that was the norm. Rome's album was not the only album being released that day.

Later on that day, Rome had a radio promotion interview scheduled to let everyone know about his album being in stores. Rome wouldn't know how many records he sold until the next day. They could go on line to Sound Scan and find out.

All day, the radios played Rome's lead single "FALLEN SOLDIERS," from the album by the same name. That was a good sign. Rome felt good riding around the city hearing his song being played from everyone's system. He even noticed that a few cars were bumping other songs from his album; another good sign.

The next day, Adonis called Rome. Rome had been resting, trying to catch up on the sleep he lost in the last couple of nights. Rome was half awake when the words Adonis spoke entered his conscious.

"You did it Rome! You have a hit album. You sold 23,854 copies on your first day. Congratulations, you are on your way to the top!" Adonis said enthusiastically.

"Are you serious? That many people went out and brought my record on the first day?"

"Yes, I'm serious."

Rome was so stunned by the good news that he couldn't speak.

"Rome, are you there?"

"I'm here. This is just great news. I'll meet you at the office at 10 o'clock." Rome hung up the phone.

Trina was in the kitchen making some breakfast. She didn't hear the conversation Rome had with Adonis, so Rome decided to play a little game with Trina.

"Adonis just called with bad news about my sells." He paused and put on a sad face. "My album is a failure." Rome hid his face in his hands to hide the smirk.

111

"Don't worry, baby. It's not over yet. That was just the first day. Your sells will pick up." Trina was rubbing his shoulders, trying to comfort him.

"I know it will catch on." Rome raised his head showing a face of joy. This confused Trina. "I was just playing with you. My album is a hit, baby. I sold 23,854 copies on the first day."

"That's great honey! I'm so happy for you." Trina hugged him tightly.

"Happy for us because when I make my first million, I'm buying us a big house on Long Island. Matter of fact, let's go celebrate. I'm taking you shopping my Queen."

For the rest of that week, the "FALLEN SOLDIERS" LP continued to sell. The album sold a total of 195,966 in the first week. Rome's whole life was about to change. In the next 6 to 12 months, he was going to work harder than he ever did in his life.

Artist Records had a tour set up for Rome. Videos for "FALLEN SOLDIERS" and a follow up single were being shot during the week; his second single off the album was "LIVING THE LIFE". It was a sure shot hit.

The sky is the limit for Rome's career. He got off to a super start. All he had to do was to keep focus and stay out of trouble. With a manager like Adonis on his side, that was easy.

Monica got a call from Fresh Faces. They finally called her after almost a month. She was cast for a rap video, but they didn't tell her the name of the artist. All they told her was the name of the director and the location of the shoot. She had to be there at 9 a.m. sharp.

When Monica arrived at the address she was given, she looked for the director, Peek Skills. He was a famous up and coming music video director. As Monica was fishing through the sea of faces, she saw a name tag that read: DIRECTOR.

"Hi, I'm Monica Pernell from Fresh Faces. I was sent here to model in your video."

Peek skills just looked at her. As he looked at her, Monica thought how much he resembled Spike Lee.

He walked around her slowly, stopping behind her and looking at her ass for about two minutes. "We   can definitely use you for the club shot and maybe as his leading lady." Peek Skills spoke in an annoying squeaky tone. "Go see the stylist over there so she can take your measurements and style your look."

Monica walked over to a Latino woman with a tag that read: STYLIST ROXY PEREZ. She looked at Monica in the same way that Peek did. Monica had to get used to the video biz.

"Hi, I'm Monica from Fresh Faces. Peek sent me over here to get some measurements."

"Yes. Stand over here for a minute." Roxy spoke with a tone and accent like Rosie Perez.

Roxy walked around her in the same slow way that Peek did. She stopped at her ass like he did also. "OK, I know what look we will create for you."

So far, Monica found the whole rap video thing a little weird. She had only been there 30 minutes and Monica thought that maybe after a couple of videos, she might like it. It took her a month to get used to stripping in front of men. This beats stripping any day!

Monica looked around the set. She observed all the equipment and people. As she was surveying the scene, she was shocked to see Adonis and Rome talking with Peek. She strolled over to greet them. "What's up honey? What are you guys doing here?"

"We're shooting a video. What are you doing here?" Adonis inquired.

"Fresh Faces sent me here to be in a video. They didn't tell me who the artist was. Just to be here at 9 o'clock. Don't tell me I'm here to be in Rome's video."

"You guessed it," Adonis said grinning.

Monica couldn't believe it. Her first video was with Rome. This is going to look good for me since Fresh Faces sent me here. Now it looks official that I do work for Fresh Faces, thought Monica.

"I get to see my Queen in action. This is going to be a day to remember," Adonis said as he touched Monica's cheek.

"It definitely will. I have to go get my make-up and styling done. I'll see you later." She kissed him on the cheek.

"That, you will." Adonis gave her the look he gives when he wants sex.

Shooting a video was a long and tedious process. To perfect thirty seconds of footage took hours of shooting. A song that was at least 5 minutes took days to finish at times.

Adonis was used to the long working hours of a video shoot. Rome and Monica were so tired by the end of the day that they both vowed to sleep a whole 24 hours. It was finally over after 13 hours of shooting.

"Man, that was some hard work right there," Rome said to Monica.

"I know, but you will have to get used to it. That was my fifteenth video shoot." Adonis spoke like a seasoned veteran. "Fortunately for me, I don't have to work in them; I just have to sit around."

"Honey, I'm exhausted." Monica leaned on his shoulder. "I don't see how they do it, video after video."

"That's the music biz. Rome has to do another one tomorrow. The only reason they didn't start it tonight was because they ran out of film," stated Adonis.

"I'm going home to rest for at least 8 hours. Can I do that?" Rome asked.

Adonis looked at his watch. It was 12:30am. "Well if you go home and fall asleep by 1 o'clock and you are back here in the morning, you will get almost 8 hours of rest."

Rome just looked at Adonis like he was crazy. He didn't bother responding.

"Baby, could you give me a massage tonight?" Monica asked Adonis.

"Yes, I can give my poor baby a massage. Come on, let's go home."

CHAPTER 12

It didn't take long before Rome became a household name. His album had reached platinum status within sixty days. The life of a rap star was hard work for Rome. He had to get used to pleasing his fans. Wherever he went, there were fans wanting to take pictures and get autographs.

It was nonstop touring for Rome. He would do like ten shows straight before he got a day or two to himself, then it was back on the road again.

He missed Trina and Tavon. Whenever he had free time, Rome spent it with them.

He bought a colonial house in Belmont, Long Island. Belmont was on the borderline of Queens. Trina loved her new house. Monica would visit her every weekend.

Trina didn't know anyone in her new neighborhood. She met a couple of mothers at the bus stop while taking Tavon to school. Other than that, she was bored in her new home. With Rome hardly ever home, Trina was even lonelier than before.

Monica's career as a video vixen took off after her first video appearance with Rome. Directors would call Fresh Faces asking for the beauty with the green eyes.

Pamela prided herself on giving Monica a chance. It paid off for the agency. Monica was a video star, which meant opportunities for other avenues in modeling. Pamela was considering Monica for runway and print work. Things were definitely looking good for Monica's new career.

On the other hand, things were not looking so good for Dexter Ring Wald Tremont, the third, a/k/a Official. His career as a rapper was finished. An anonymous caller contacted a popular rap radio station and said some things about Official. The caller aired out all of Official secrets.

"Official is the biggest trick in the world. He isn't from no hood, and ladies, he is not holding like he says. He is a little dick lame. He thinks he is the shit. He is the shit all right; he is a piece of shit." The caller spoke in a nasty tone.

The news about Official spread like wildfire in a forest. All the women he dated began to come forward to confirm what the first caller said. Women he dated three years ago were telling their stories. *The Source, Vibe and the XXL* magazines aired articles about the rumors. Every rap outlet was capitalizing on Official's downfall.

The stories of Official were the talk of the town. His record label was even talking about dropping him. The negative press was too degrading. They were afraid that it would reflect on them.

All of the negative press killed the sales of his new album. His first album went double platinum. The second one went double copper. You couldn't pay someone to buy his album. Official became the laughing stock of the industry. Even the new rappers took shots at him on their mix tapes. He quickly went from having it all to a has-been overnight.

He had an idea who was to blame for all of this, or at least he thought he knew. There was only one person he could think of who threatened to tell the truth about him. That person was Monica a/k/a Banana Pudding, the new rap video queen. Dexter vowed to get her back if it was the last thing he does.

Everyone in the rap industry knew who Monica Pernell was. They knew she had a man in the industry. They were always together at industry events. Whenever you saw one, you saw the other. Their relationship was no secret.

Men are going to be men. Guys still tried to get at Monica despite them knowing Adonis. Some of them knew Adonis personally, but still wanted a taste of her Banana Pudding. Monica would never cheat on her King. He was her everything and she didn't need anyone else.

One day while Adonis was at his office, he got a call from Official. Adonis was busy, but Official insisted that it was important. "What is it Dexter? I'm very busy, make it fast."

"I just thought you should know about Monica. You and I have always been cool and..." Adonis cut him off mid-sentence.

"I know, but get to the point Dexter, I'm busy."

"Your girl is a stripper named Banana Pudding. She strips at Sue's Rendezvous."

"Yeah right, everyone knows that Monica is the most sought after video chick in the industry. Look Dexter, just because you're a has-been, don't call me with some bullshit about my Queen. Now, if you'll excuse me, I have work to do." Adonis slammed the phone down so that Dexter would get the message.

After Adonis hung up the phone, he thought about what Dexter told him. A stripper named Banana Pudding? That sounds like some made up shit, thought Adonis. After thinking some more, something in the back of his mind was telling him that it could be true. Adonis remembered the night at the album release party how Monica was dancing and how she used to sleep all day. It was eating him up just thinking about the possibility of his Queen as Banana Pudding.

Adonis had more thoughts about the call and concluded that he would face the music. What am I bugging out for? All I have to do is ask her. I'm sure she was not Banana Pudding. Later that night, they were alone at Adonis's brownstone watching a movie. Adonis decided to ask her about the Banana Pudding fiasco that Dexter spoke about.

Monica practically lived with Adonis now. She basically kept her condo because Adonis didn't have enough closet space for her.

Monica noticed that Adonis had something on his mind. Whatever it was, it was troubling him. She learned his different mind states from spending so much time with him. Since Adonis was such a positive person, he seldom had attitudes. When he did get an attitude, it was for a genuine reason.

"Is there something on your mind?"

Adonis looked her in the eyes so he could detect the slightest inclination of a lie when he questioned her.

"Does the name Banana Pudding mean anything to you?"

The look that came over Monica's face at the mere utterance of the words Banana Pudding told Adonis that it did. She didn't' even have to say a word. Her facial expression said it all. She turned her head away from him. She couldn't take the heat that his stare gave off.

A feeling of pain struck Adonis' heart like a lightning bolt. He could not believe that Dexter was telling the truth.

All this time I thought she was a model and she was a stripper; the lowest women on earth, Adonis thought.

Adonis got up from the couch. Monica tried to grab his arm. He snatched it from her. "Don't touch me!" He shouted loud enough to wake Makeda. "You're a stripper! All this time you've been lying to me. I cannot believe this shit!"

Monica never saw Adonis like this. He never used profanity and he never raised his voice. He was always in control of his emotions.

"I'm not a stripper." She paused. "Not anymore."

"What do you mean *not anymore*?" He sounded confused. "How long ago? When did you stop? And please do not lie to me."

Monica was silent, thinking about what she should say to him. She was going to tell him the truth. "I stopped four months ago."

"Four months ago! We have been together for a year now. So what you're telling me is up until four months ago, you were a stripper named Banana Pudding?"

Monica saw the hurt on his face. It hurt her to be the cause of his pain. The thought that she hurt the one man she has ever loved, made her cry. She cried like someone that just lost a loved one.

"Please get out of my house." He spoke to her with authority, something he had never done.

"But Adonis, I'm not a stripper anymore. I stopped for you. I love you." She spoke through tears.

"You lied to me. How can you love me?"

"I swear to you, Adonis. I fell in love with you from the first time I laid eyes on you. That's the only reason I lied to you."

Adonis was thinking about everything. He thought how about how they met and all of the experiences they shared. He remembered the time when Monica asked him about her friend who was a stripper. He now knew that she was talking about herself.

"You knew how I felt about strippers. You should have told me the day you asked me about your friend. Now I know you were talking about yourself." Adonis was crying. He couldn't take it anymore. "Just leave, Monica. I don't ever want to see you again."

He opened the front door.

"Can we talk about this?"

Adonis just stood at the door. His gesture said *get out* without any words.

Monica put on her shoes and her coat and left the brownstone. Monica's whole world had just collapsed. She walked blindly without looking at the street names. Rain started to pour down as she walked. She didn't care. She just walked.

She was so numb that nothing could medicate her emotions. She walked that way for two hours. Monica got tired and caught a cab to her condo.

When she got in the condo, she cried for hours until she fell asleep. When she woke up the next day, Monica had a cold from being out in the rain. Along with her congested chest and runny nose, she had a broken heart.

I can't believe the only man I ever loved just dumped me. He had a good reason to; I lied to him. I deceived him for eight months. I would have left me too. Fuck that. I'm not going to let him go that easily. I'm not going to let my King go without a fight. I'm the Queen on this chess board, and this is the chess board of life.

Monica picked up the phone and called Adonis's office. His secretary said that he didn't come in today. "He said that he wasn't feeling good," The secretary informed Monica.

She called his brownstone, but there was no answer. She knew he was there. She got into her BMW and sped off towards his house. Monica was determined to state her case to him.

She still had the keys to his brownstone. She didn't have to knock to get in. When she entered, Adonis was sitting on the couch with a blanket around his head and shoulders, pretending to watch TV. He had a blank stare on his face. His eyes were puffy and red like he had been up all night crying. He looked like he had lost his best friend. In his mind, he did lose his best friend.

"We are going to talk, whether you want to or not," Monica demanded.

Adonis didn't respond to her. He ignored her as if she wasn't even there.

"Damn it Adonis! You are going to listen to me. I know you fucking hear me!"

122

She felt like smacking him in the face to get his attention, but he turned his head towards her. He gave her a look that almost brought tears to her eyes. She remained strong and spoke with conviction.

"I'm so very sorry for lying to you. You really don't know how much pain I'm in right now. I want to explain something to you. I didn't lie to you to hurt you. I lied to you because I was ashamed of what I was. That day we met, I knew you were special. I know how most men view strippers, so I lied to give myself a chance to get to know you." She paused to see if he was listening. His eyes said that he was.

"I didn't grow up like you did. I didn't have two loving parents or lived in a nice home or lived in a good neighborhood. I grew up in do or die Bedford-Stuyvesant, Brooklyn. My parents were both heroin addicts. Many nights I went to bed starving because the money for food was in their veins. My neighborhood was a drug infested war zone with gunshots all day and night. People were getting killed right in front of you. You learned survival early. Only the strong survive."

Monica waited for Adonis to respond. When he didn't, she continued her plea.

"I learned the lessons of the streets at a very young age, not because I wanted to, but because I had to. Everyone had to have a hustle or you didn't eat. It was as simple as that. My looks and my body always got me over, so I learned to use them. That's what led me to be a stripper since I was 18 years old. I didn't do it because I liked it...I did it to survive. I tried working a regular job, but the money I got from stripping was addictive."

123

After a short pause, Monica continued, "Then you came into my life. You were the best thing that happened to me. Because of you, I know I'm a Queen. I know I'm worth more than a stripper. It is because of you that I'm not stripping anymore. No man has enlightened me the way you have. For that, I am most thankful. I don't want to lose you, Adonis. Please forgive me. I promise you I will never lie to you again."

Monica was crying as she spoke. Her speech was so sincere that Adonis had no choice, but to feel this beautiful woman in front of him. He understood where she was from. Even though he was from the suburbs, he understood the Black struggle.

Adonis couldn't help but to shed a tear. The moment was so emotional that he couldn't stop the tears from falling. He looked at his Queen. He really loved her.

"Come here, my Queen."

Monica fell into his arms and they engaged in an air tight lover's embrace. "I love you so much, Adonis," Monica said as she cried on his chest.

"I love you more my Queen."

"No, I love you more."

"I said it first, so I'm the originator of loving more." Adonis cleverly won the match.

They kissed and held each other for the whole day. They made passionate love that night. Make up sex is always the best.

Things between Adonis and Monica had never been better. With all her skeletons out of the closet, Monica felt enormous relief. Thanks to fake ass Dexter, Monica thought to herself.

Little did Monica know, Dexter wasn't finished with his attempts to destroy her. He was sure that Monica was the one who started the campaign to destroy his career. Dexter went public with his story about the New Rap Video Queen, Monica Pernell. He told reporters how she was a stripper named Banana Pudding before becoming a Rap Video Queen. He told them how she used to sell sex. He admitted to spending money on her.

The scandal didn't get as much negative publicity as the story on him received. It did make enough noise to get back to Fresh Faces. They were considering letting her go, but somehow the news boosted Monica's popularity. Fresh Faces received so many requests for her that she became the hardest working model in their stable.

Adonis was furious about what Dexter was doing to his Queen. "When I see Dexter, I'm going to pummel his ass."

"Don't even waste your time. I can beat him up myself." Monica said. "Besides, my Publicist advised me to go public with it because his scheme is backfiring on his dumb ass. He just made me ten times more popular. I'm the most requested model at Fresh Faces. Thank you, Official, I mean Dexter, for boosting my career."

Monica had an interview with Winny Williams, the number one radio talk show host. She was about to tell her side of the story. Everyone wanted to listen to what she had to say.

"We are here today with Monica 'Banana Pudding' Pernell. She is the most sought after rap video model in America and she is the topic of a scandal headed by has-been rapper, Official." Winny didn't like Official. "Now Monica, tell us your side of the story."

"I dated Dexter, but not for money. I did meet him when I was working at Sue's, but I only liked him because he was very popular at the time. Dexter is trying to slander me because we had a fall out and he thought I was the caller who first exposed him. Dexter, I hope you are listening right now. I did not call any radio station and blow your fake ass up. One of your other chicks did that. I don't have time to think about you. But since you thought it was me, and you drew first blood, I'm here to defend myself. I can confirm that everything the sisters said about you is the truth. So Dexter, please get a life. "

That interview was aired everywhere. This was the missile that sank Official's ship. Dexter Ring Wald Tremont, the Third, also known as Official, was officially a has-been.

All the press about the new rap Video Queen made Monica a sex symbol. That brought her more work. She didn't strip anymore. Her new fans fantasized that she did. She was booked up for work for the whole year.

Dexter still had a chance as a rapper, just not in America. Official had a small following in Canada. He moved to Toronto where the stories of his lameness didn't follow.

He signed a record deal with a major Canadian record label and he ended up selling thousands of records there. He stuck to the script. In Canada, he was a thug, a pimp and everything when he was in his prime in America. That was until he was defeated by Banana Pudding.

126

The truth will always come to the light. Soon the women in Canada will figure out that he is a phony. It is what it is.

CHAPTER 13

Meanwhile, back in Bedford-Stuyvesant on Quincy Ave., Big Walt was becoming a ghetto super star. Since Rome and PT discontinued their drug dynasty, it was all his. Big Walt became the man that everyone went to for their weight. He was getting money like never before.

Big Walt was also an avid hater of Rome. He was not only a member, but he was the Hater President of the Rome Hater's Club.

"Turn that motherfucking shit off in my car," Big Walt would demand from anyone who listened to the radio in his car when Rome's music came on. The DJ's played Rome's music so much in NYC that Big Walt stopped listening to the radio. Big Walt had developed a deep hatred for Rome and his success as a rapper.

One day, Big Walt came home to find his girl and her friends watching rap videos. They had the TV stereo up so loud that they didn't hear Walt come in. One of Rome's videos came on. Walt was furious because he told Tasha not to play Rome's music in his house. He started to spaz-out right then and there, but he heard them talking about Rome and eavesdropped on the ladies.

"That's Rome from Gates Ave. His shit is the hottest shit out. Oh, I forgot your man don't want you playing Rome's music in his house," said one of the women.

"Yeah, but I still listen to it though. Walt is stupid. Plus Rome is cute. Money makes a motherfucker look good, right?" Tasha said raising her hand in the air.

"Mm-hmm, sure do girl," her friend said slapping Tasha's hand in the air.

Big Walt couldn't take it anymore. He was fuming now. He came from behind the wall like a mad bull. "Get all of your stank asses out of my fucking house!" He yelled at the top of his lungs. "Yeah, all of you stank ass ho's, get the fuck out of here and don't let me catch you in here again!"

The girls quickly got up and ran for the door.

"You think he's cute, bitch!" he yelled in Tasha's face.

"Come on Walt! Stop bugging."

Walt punched Tasha in the face so hard that her ears were ringing.

"You want to fuck him, too, with your nasty ass!"

BAM! Walt hit her again, this time instantly blacking her eye.

"Why are you hitting me?" she protested through swollen and bloody lips. She tried to run past Walt, but he grabbed her arm and flung her to the floor.

"Get your ass in the room and don't come out till I say."

Tasha ran into the room, slammed the door, and locked it. She lied on the bed and cried.

As time went on, Big Walt's hatred for Rome got worse. He hated Rome with a passion. It would not have been so bad if Rome wasn't such a huge celebrity. Everywhere Walt went he was reminded of how successful Rome had become. Rome had giant posters of himself all over the five boroughs of NYC. Rome even had a huge billboard of himself on Atlantic Avenue.

Big Walt was green with envy over Rome's career. He was mad because Rome was the man. He made it out of the drug game. If he ever saw Rome back in the hood, he would probably shoot him himself out of a jealous rage.

Walt had heard that Rome moved to a big house out in Long Island. No one knew where it was. Walt would like to know where it was. He wanted to bomb it to smithereens.

There was nothing that Big Walt could do about Rome's success but handle it. There was no sign that Rome's career was about to fall. He kept coming out with more and more hits.

Rome was about to drop his second album. His first one went double platinum. He had guest appearances on everyone's album. Big Walt began to hate the other artists that Rome affiliated with. The degree of success that Rome had achieved made Big Walt's head hurt sometimes.

Big Walt had moved up to selling keys, which meant he was hood rich. Hood rich means you have over $100,000. In the hood, you would be considered a hood millionaire. A new rival came with Big Walt's new found drug empire. His name was Stack Money, or Stack for short.

Stack was a money-getting thug who got a name back in the days for robbing everything that moved. He went upstate to do five years. When he came home, he switched his hustle from robbing to selling drugs. He was still known for busting his guns, but he let it cool off to get drug money.

Stack and Rambo were cronies. They knew each other from the streets and they were also upstate together. Whenever two guys do time together, they have a bond. The bond is based on understanding incarceration.

Stack knew Rome, too. He liked to see a brother from the hood make it in the music business. Stack wasn't a hater, he was a "congratulator".

Rome tried to pull Rambo off the streets and take him on tour with him. Rambo loved the streets. He was the type of guy who was raised on the streets. Eventually, he was going to die on the streets. Rambo was only home one month before he reverted back to a life of crime. He wanted to open up the spot that Rome and PT left behind.

"Yo, Stack, I want to put some work on Gates Ave. That bitch ass nigga Walt from Quincy Ave. is getting all the money. Quiet as kept, Walt killed PT. Rome was meant to die that day, too." Rambo spoke with a criminal expression.

"Word. I was never feeling that bitch ass nigga since back in the days when he used to think he was a bully."

"You know I don't give a fuck. I don't see why Walt should be getting all the money."

"Bet, starting tomorrow I'm going to set up shop with you on Gates Ave. Let's get this money," Stack said.

Rambo and Stack had plans to cut into Walt's cheese the same way Rome and PT did. This time they were going to bring it to Big Walt first before he gets a chance to get them. Stack and Rambo were seasoned vets in the game. Stack had the drugs, so it wasn't going to take long before they took over Walt's business.

That next day, they set up shop. For the first week business was slow. By the third week, Stack and Rambo were seeing thousands. Big Walt had built up a nice clientele for them to take from him.

Another thing that Big Walt didn't know was that Stack had a spy in his midst. Stack and Rambo knew everything that Big Walt was doing. The spy that Stack had planted in Walt's midst was someone who was close to him. Walt was sleeping with the enemy. His girl, Tasha, was secretly sleeping with Stack.

Stack and Tasha had a history together. They were together before her and Big Walt became an item. Tasha used to be Stack's girl before he got locked up. When he went upstate, she couldn't handle it, so she moved on. She still had feelings for Stack.

Stack wasn't mad at her. He understood her decision. Stack was a real gentleman when it came to women. He never hit a woman or even raised his voice to a woman.

Stack was a gangster and a gentleman. Tasha was attracted to his thug side and his gentle side. Tasha saw tough men cower in his presence. She saw how much respect he demanded on the streets. She remembered one incident when a couple was arguing. The man started beating on his woman. Stack grabbed the man's hand and said, "Son, you don't have to beat her like that." He spoke calmly.

"Who the fuck is you? Nigga, if you don't take your hand off of me."

His words stopped and extreme fear showed on his face. He was staring down the barrel of Stack's .45.

"What you gonna do? Nothing! Just like I thought, you're not so tough now. Get the fuck out of here."

The man ran off and left his girl standing there.

"That was very heroic of you, Stack," Tasha said about his actions.

"A real man doesn't hit women. Men who hit women are cowards," said Stack.

Tasha reflected on those memories of when she was with Stack. She compared him to Big Walt.

Stack is a real man, unlike that fat slob Walt. I wish I was still Stack's girl, Tasha thought.

Those memories of Stack made it easy for Tasha to except his offer to rekindle the fire. She enjoyed being sneaky to Big Walt because he beat her. This was her way of getting even with him. Besides, she really liked Stack. She was starting to hate Big Walt with a passion.

Stack still had feelings for Tasha, but he was using her. He needed to find out bits of info about Big Walt's business. At first, he never asked Tasha any questions about Big Walt. They just caught up on old times. They laughed and made love like old times.

After he got her trust, Stack began to ask questions about Big Walt to see if she would talk. Sometimes, hustlers keep their women in the dark about business. That was Big Walt's mistake. He let Tasha know all of his business.

"How do you put up with that fat bastard?" Stack asked. He watched her reaction closely. "I know why, because he got money. How much money does Walt make?"

"I know he makes like twenty thousand in a week. He bags a key of coke every week and he sells the rest in weight."

That was too easy. I just asked one question, Stack thought. Stack would plant seeds of hatred in her head. It would be easy to get her to set him up. She continued to answer questions about Big Walt's business affairs. Stack was waiting for the right time.

Tasha was falling back in love with Stack. He was the total opposite of Walt. She felt protected around Stack. She never felt protected by Walt; furthermore, she needed protection from him. The beatings continued and Tasha wanted to leave him. She didn't have anywhere to go, so she stayed.

On one of her rendezvous with Stack, he noticed she was wearing big, dark shades. He took them off and saw a black eye. He was furious. He started to like Tasha.

"That bitch ass nigga hit you again? That's it. I'm going to take care of him once and for all."

Tasha didn't protest. Someone needed to do something about him.

"This is what I need to know. Where does he keep the money?" Stack asked.

"He keeps it in a safe in the closet."

"OK, tonight I want you to unlock the door at exactly 2 a.m. You understand me? 2 a.m. He is going to get a rude awakening tonight."

Stack told Rambo about his plans to rob Big Walt. He even came up with a brilliant idea. He thought it would be best if they disguised themselves as Cagney and Lacey. They were known to wear wigs and trench coats. Rambo thought it was a good idea, too.

134

"Yeah, we can dress up like those two bitches who he hired to kill Rome and PT."

"Exactly."

The time had finally come for the job. It was 1:45 am. Stack and Rambo were anxious to rob and kill Walt. Stack wanted him dead because he was falling in love with Tasha. Rambo wanted to kill him for PT.

Stack and Rambo looked ridiculously comical in their wigs and trench coats. Stack wore a red wig that almost looked orange. Rambo wore a blond wig that resembled one Lil Kim wore. Both men looked at each other and almost passed out from laughter. After they got off the long laugh, it was time for business.

When they got to Walt's third floor apartment, Stack checked the door. It was open just like Tasha said it would be. They tiptoed in, went straight to the bed room, and turned on the lights. Tasha was already awake. When she saw the two men wearing wigs and dark glasses, she had to cover her mouth to stop herself from laughing.

A minute later, Big Walt awoke. "Bitch, if you don't turn that motherfucking light off!" He lifted his head and saw Rambo and Stack standing there wearing wigs, holding guns.

Walt turned his head to the side in confusion. He focused in on the men and started laughing. The laughter was quiet at first but it got louder because everyone joined in. Walt covered his eyes to block the comic view in front of him. When he removed his hand, the laughter became so loud and hilarious that it was contagious.

Walt couldn't control himself. He laughed so hard that he began to cry. Tasha began to tear from laughter

135

also. They all laughed so hard that Stack and Rambo almost forgot why they were there. Then Stack tapped Rambo on the shoulder and they stopped laughing. This was no laughing matter.

"Ok motherfucker, jokes over. Open the fucking safe!" Stack said with the seriousness of a killer.

Walt stopped laughing and assessed the situation He looked at Rambo with the blond wig on and thought how he resembled an ugly Lil' Kim. He started to laugh again. Though this was no laughing matter, the sight of these two men in wigs was funny. He laughed until Rambo's gun butted him twice in the head.

"This shit isn't funny now. Is it? Now open up the fucking safe!"

Walt immediately stopped laughing and almost started crying. He got up from the bed and went into the closet to open the safe.

If I can grab the .45, Walt thought. Walt had a loaded .45 caliber in the safe. Walt opened the safe and tried to reach in as if he was grabbing cash. He got his hand on the .45. When he brought it out, Stack saw the glare of the gun off the light. Before Walt could get his hand out of the safe with the .45, BANG! BANG! Stack hit him twice in the back of his head, sending pieces of brain and blood onto the money in the safe.

The money in the safe was soaked in Walt's blood.

"Damn Stack, you got blood all over the money," Rambo Said.

"Fuck it, it's still good. Now it's really blood money."

They filled up duffle bags with the blood money.

136

"In twenty minutes, call the police and tell them what happened. Remember to describe us as two females with wigs on," Stack said to Tasha. Stack had instructed her on what to do the night before.

As they were leaving, one of the neighbors called the cops. "I heard gunshots next door. When I looked I saw two women running out wearing wigs," the neighbor said.

Stack and Rambo ran into an alley and took off the wigs and trench coats. They threw them in a dumpster and walked out normally like nothing happened.

When they got to Stacks house, they emptied the money onto a round kitchen table. It took them almost two hours to count the money twice.

Stack said, "$220,000 dollars. Fastest money I ever made." They gave each other handshakes of congratulations.

"I think I might buy this CL550 Benz I saw on Atlantic Ave," Rambo said.

"We should wait a week before we start spending," Stack replied.

Rambo was thinking very grimy now. He didn't want to show his thoughts to Stack. He had larceny in his heart. He wanted to kill Stack and take all the money. He knew Stack was a vet and he would be on point.

"You think we should have killed the chick? She might get funny on us and tell the police," warned Rambo.

"No man, she hated Walt's guts. He used to beat her ass. I told her I was going to kill him. I might kill her later on."

"I'll kill the bitch if you want. I know you won't. I know you like her a little."

"Fuck it, kill her this weekend. I want to fuck her one last time. She got some good pussy," said Stack. He was fronting. He didn't really want Rambo to kill Tasha. He had developed deep feelings for her. She was a good girl.

Stack had a plan. He would tell her that Rambo was going to kill her, and that she should skip town. He would give her $15,000 for her role in the caper. If Rambo couldn't find her, he couldn't kill her.

Stack understood why Rambo wanted to kill her. He couldn't let it happen. Stack would've killed her if he was Rambo. Stack had to admit it to himself, that he loved Tasha. He wasn't going to tell Rambo that.

Rambo wasn't stupid. He knew that Stack loved Tasha. That's why Rambo was going to get it over with before Stack could stop him. There was no honor amongst thieves. Stack knew that, too. He knew that Rambo was a grimy dude. That's why Stack stayed two steps ahead of him.

At the 79th precinct, Detectives Brown and Santiago were going over the facts of the latest murder connected to Cagney and Lacey. They knew that the original Lacey was dead.

"Maybe Cagney recruited a new partner," Santiago suggested.

"I don't know. You have to think. Why would she get another partner? She wouldn't trust just anyone. Something doesn't add up with this one. I think it is a copy-cat job."

"We have two witnesses who say for sure it was two females with wigs on. That fits Cagney's MO to the tee," Santiago suggested.

"Yeah, maybe you're right, partner. But my instincts are telling me otherwise," said Brown.

Santiago learned in the past how his veteran partner's instincts were 90% right, so Santiago didn't dismiss Brown's notions.

"Something about the girlfriend didn't sit right with me. She was too calm, too nonchalant when she was telling her story. Her boyfriend just got his brains blown out and she wasn't crying," reported Brown in a suspicious tone.

"You're right. I got that same feeling last night when we went to question her," agreed Santiago.

"There was no forced entry. The door wasn't off the hinges or anything. Which means the door was either left unlocked or Walt opened the door for them. Knowing Walt's history, he had too many enemies to leave his door unlocked."

"So you think that the girlfriend got this setup somehow?" Santiago asked.

"It's very possible. Maybe we should get her down here for more questions. She may bust under pressure," Brown said while looking at his partner for an agreement. When he nodded, Brown and Santiago headed towards Walt's apartment to get Tasha.

Rambo was sitting across the street from Walt's apartment building. He was waiting for Tasha to come out, or he was going in. Either way, he was determined to kill her today. Rambo couldn't sleep, thinking that she would tell the police what really happened.

Fuck waiting till the weekend. I'm killing this bitch today, Rambo thought to himself.

Tasha was inside the apartment getting her things together to move. The apartment spooked her. She couldn't live there anymore. She got a call from Stack. Her heart was racing when she saw his name on her caller ID.

"Tasha, listen to me very closely. Come to my apartment immediately. I can't tell you on the phone why, but it's very important. Come right now." Stack abruptly hung up the phone.

Tasha put on a jacket and walked out of the apartment building. She was moving at a fast pace. Whatever it was that Stack had to tell her, she knew it was important. Stack was a very serious person. If he told a person that it was important, that's what it was. She wanted to be with him, anyway. This urgent situation just gave her a reason.

Rambo watched Tasha as she stepped out of the building. He was in the cut. She didn't even see him. He followed her from across the street.

At the same time that Rambo followed her, Brown and Santiago were pulling up.

"Let's apprehend her," Santiago said.

Brown suggested, "I have a better idea. Let's follow her for a few blocks and see where she leads us." Santiago shook his head in agreement.

As Brown and Santiago followed Tasha, they noticed a guy crossing the street, walking quickly up to her.

"That may be somebody connected to the crime," Brown said when he noticed Rambo.

What they saw next was traumatizing. Rambo pulled out a 357 magnum. BANG! BANG! He shot Tasha twice right behind her left ear.

"Oh shit!" Santiago said.

Brown got on the radio. "A woman was just shot walking on Quincy Ave between Marcus Garvey and Troop! Send an ambulance ASAP!"

Santiago was driving the car. He sped up to Rambo. Rambo looked at his side and saw the detectives moving fast towards him.

"Oh shit, the Dee's!" Rambo said to himself when he realized who they were.

"Let me out. I'll chase him on foot," Brown said.

Brown was no slow-foot cop. Rambo felt the man on his heels. Rambo let off two shots without looking back. Brown continued to run, bending to dodge the oncoming bullets. Rambo let off five more rounds at Brown.

Brown let off five rounds of his own. All five hit Rambo in his back, from the base of his spine, to the stem of his brain.

Rambo was dead on arrival. Brown was an expert marksman. The bullets hit him with precision.

Tasha was dead. Rambo was dead. The case was dead.

Brown knew that without Tasha, they had no leads. He would bet his career that the suspect he just killed was one half of the duo that killed Walt.

Stack became impatient, so he took a ride to Quincy Ave. to get Tasha himself. He saw yellow tape and the police taking pictures when he arrived. He parked his car and walked up the block.

Stack saw a young girl standing on the block.

"What happened here?" Stack asked the girl.

"Big Walt's girl, Tasha, got shot in the head by some guy. Then the guy got shot up by the police up the block." The girl spoke like a ghetto reporter.

Rambo just couldn't wait to kill Tasha. In the process, you got your dumb ass killed, too, Stack thought.

Stack felt guilty about her death. He felt like it was his fault for bringing her into it. If I wouldn't have talked her into setting up Walt, none of this would've happened. I'm through with this shit. I'm tired of destroying people's lives. I'm out of Brooklyn. I'm going to North Carolina.

Stack got into his car and left the scene. He didn't know how much the cops knew. He wasn't going to stick around to find out.

"Good bye, Tasha. I'm sorry."

Stack hit the Belt Parkway and headed towards the Verrazano Bridge. He paid his toll and never looked back.

CHAPTER 14

When Rome came home from touring, he heard about what happened to Big Walt, Tasha, and Rambo. Rome didn't know if Stack was involved, but word on the street was that Rambo and Stack opened up shop on Gates Ave. He didn't put it past Stack to be involved in the whole caper.

Rome heard about Big Walt's habitual hating. Someone who hates you that much will kill you eventually, Rome thought.

Rome was just happy to be blessed enough to be away from all the bullshit on the streets. That's exactly what the streets offered--bullshit; all of it, the drugs, the killing, and the hating, all for what? Absolutely nothing. No one got anything out of it in the end.

The streets have no love for anyone. The streets were cold. You think that the streets respect you, but the streets respect nothing or no one. You are fooling yourself if you think otherwise.

Rome understood that now. He got joy from watching his son grow up. He got joy from making Trina happy and making his mother proud.

Rome felt like he owes most of his new found mentality to Adonis. Adonis was a major factor in helping Rome change his life. Adonis taught him lots about being a Black Man. He taught him how to have good work ethics. If Adonis wasn't so hard on Rome from the beginning, Rome would have messed up his chances of success.

Rome loved Adonis like a big brother. He was more than just a manager to him. Things could not have been better in Rome's life. He had the number one album in the country. He had over a million in the bank. His family was taken care of and his career showed no signs of slowing down.

The house was empty when Rome got in. "Where is Trina?" he asked himself. "Let me call her up," he took out his cell phone and dialed Trina.

She answered, "Hi Boo. Are you home?"

"Yes I'm home. Where are you at?"

"I'm at the Green Acres mall with Monica and the kids," Trina replied.

"I'll be here sleeping when you come home."

"OK Boo. I'll see you in a few."

Trina and Monica did a lot of shopping these days. Their men were not cheap men. Plus, Monica made much money modeling, more than stripping ever made her. She appreciated being able to let people know her profession. Today, she found out some good news that she wanted to share with Trina.

"Trina, do you notice anything different about me?" Monica asked. Trina looked her up and down before answering.

"Nothing, except your head got bigger." Trina said jokingly. "What am I supposed to notice?"

"You're so stupid. Seriously, Trina." Monica smiled and her cheeks had a slight glow to them.

"Monica, are you pregnant?" asked Trina with a big smile on her face.

144

"Yes, I am. I found out this morning. My period was a month late. The way me and Adonis go at it, I knew it would happen sooner or later."

Trina hugged Monica. She was almost in tears. "I'm so happy for you. I'm going to be an aunt. Makeda is going to have a brother."

"How do you know it's a boy?" asked Monica with a perplexed look on her face.

"I just know. Did you tell Adonis yet?"

"No. I'm going to tell him tonight. He has been talking about having a baby lately. This morning, he was so tired that he was late for work. You know what they say about your man being extra tired? I knew right there that I was pregnant."

"I can't wait till you have this baby. Both of you are pretty so I know the baby is going to be pretty."

Monica was trying to imagine how their baby would look. She got lost in space thinking about it.

Trina watched while Monica daydreamed.

"Monica! Snap out of it. You never changed. You've been daydreaming like that since we were in third grade. I used to think you were retarded or something." Trina was only playing with her.

"Stop playing. You know I wasn't retarded. I used to get better grades than you."

"Did you hear about what happened to Big Walt from Quincy?" Trina asked.

"No. What happened?"

"He was murdered. And the next day his girl, Tasha, was killed by Rambo. The cops were on the scene when Rambo shot Tasha, so they chased him down and he shot at the cops. The cops shot back and hit Rambo in the back of his head."

"Damn, shit is still off the hook around there. I'm glad I got the hell out of there," said Monica.

"Me too."

The girls finished their shopping and parted ways. When Monica got home, Adonis was on the couch dozing off. He heard her enter the house and he woke up.

"Oh, hi honey. I was about to take a nap. I've been really tired all day. Maybe I need to take some vitamins."

"I know why you are tired," stated Monica in a quiet voice.

Adonis sat up when she said that.

"The same reason that I'm tired," said Monica. Monica sat down next to him while she stared into his eyes. She was trying to see a baby's face in his.

"You're tired, too? Must be all the love we've been making." Adonis gave her a sexy smile.

"That has something to do with it."

Adonis knew what she was hinting at. He was just waiting for her to say it. "Adonis, I'm pregnant. We're having a baby."

Adonis hugged Monica so tightly that she was gasping for air. "Adonis, I can't breathe."

"I'm so sorry, I was just... Wow! This is great news, baby. I can't believe it. Do you need anything? Here, relax and put your feet up."

Monica laughed at the way he was acting. She had never seen him like this. He was the same way when Tammy was pregnant with Makeda. He would wait on her hand and foot. It got so bad that Tammy had to tell him to relax.

Monica thought it was cute the way Adonis catered to her, but she would soon start to feel like Tammy.

A couple of months went by and Adonis continued to "baby" Monica. It began to annoy her. Sometimes he acted as though she couldn't even walk without him following her.

"Are you Ok? Do you need anything? Can I get you anything?" He repeated the same questions a million times a day. Monica tolerated it with a smile. He meant well, so she just let him wait on her hand and foot.

Makeda was lots of help with Monica also. She would talk to her stomach all the time. "I don't know if you're my little brother or my little sister. Whatever you are, I'm going to show you the ropes when you come out."

Monica thought that was the cutest thing she had ever seen. Makeda would talk to Monica's stomach so much that whenever the baby heard her voice, it started kicking inside.

Makeda was such a smart young girl. She was destined to be something great in life. She had that natural charm and charisma that the greats have. Those are the qualities that are detected at a young age.

Makeda was only seven years old, but she was a mature seven. She was seven going on seventeen. She already had a savings account that she operated herself. When her monthly statements came in the mail she knew how to read them. She put $25 in her account every week. She had $2,225 in her account.

"By the time I'm eighteen, I should have almost $20,000 saved. Plus, with interest, it will be more," stated Makeda with certainty.

"I think you'll have more than that at eighteen. Knowing you, you'll have a job making money by the time you're twelve," said Monica.

"Come to think of it, you're right, Monica. I can work for my Daddy."

Adonis had a surprise for Monica tonight. They were going to a dinner party at Rome's house in Long Island. He was going to propose to her at the dinner party. The only person he told was Rome. He showed Rome the 5-carat diamond ring he bought for her.

"You paid *some* money for that," Rome said with admiration.

"She is worth every penny of it, and more."

On the night of the dinner party, Adonis was quiet. He was a little nervous. His plan was to start a conversation with her and then surprise her with the question.

Monica was six months pregnant now. The sonogram said it was a boy. The name they agreed on was Adonis Nkosi, Junior. Adonis had no qualms with that. In fact, he loved the idea of having a Jr.

After everyone ate and settled down, Adonis sat next to Monica. "You know something, Monica. I really love you, and there is something I want to ask you."

Adonis stood up and spoke loudly so everyone could hear him. "Excuse me everyone. May I have your attention? I have an announcement to make." He paused and turned to Monica. "Monica, I fell in love with you from the very first time I saw you. When I got to know you, I fell deeper in love. You are my perfect idea of what a Queen is. I love you more than anything. I want to be with you for the rest of my days. I don't ever want us to be apart. I want to know." He paused to pull out the ring box from his pocket. "Monica, will you marry me?" He opened up the ring box and took out the princess-cut diamond engagement ring. He placed it on her finger.

One look at the ring and her breathing became sporadic. Even the baby inside Monica knew something was going on because he was kicking.

Monica's eyes filled up with tears. She was overwhelmed with joy. "Yes! Yes I will gladly marry you, Adonis Nkosi." She hugged him so tight the bones in his back cracked. Everyone clapped and gave them praise and congratulations.

It was a very joyous occasion for everyone. The joy that Monica and Adonis radiated had vibrated into everyone at the dinner. There were six adults and fours kids present at the dinner. This was Monica and Adonis' night.

Monica must have told Adonis she loved him a million times. Her ring was shining like a miniature sun. Monica knew diamonds, and from the color, cut and clarity, her ring was flawless.

"That ring is beautiful, girl," Trina said. "That shit is blinding me."

"Me,too. That shit look like a flashlight," Fat Tommy's wife, Vita, said.

All of the women gathered in their circle. They were talking about the things that women talk about. Most of the conversation was about Monica's ring and her baby.

"It is good to walk a lot when you are pregnant. It lessens the labor pain," Rena said.

"She is right. I didn't do anything but lie around and eat. I was in labor with Imhotep for Twelve hours," Vita said.

"It is hard for me to do anything with Adonis around. Every time I move, he asks me if I'm OK or do I want anything. I had to tell him that I was OK."

The women continued their chat.

The men were in their own little circle. They talked about everything that most men talk about; sports, cars, careers, and their families. Since all of these men were in the music industry, they spoke mostly about that.

"I heard that Dexter, I mean, Official took his show on the road, literally. He supposed to be hot up in Canada," Fat Tommy said.

"Oh yeah, I should call my people up there and blow his spot up again. He tried to disrespect my Queen. He's lucky he moved somewhere because I was going to hit him so hard he'd wish he would have moved," Adonis said. All the men laughed and continued conversing.

"How is your label doing, Lance?" Fat Tommy asked.

"We have a great distribution deal set with Omni. Our artists are pretty hot. With the help of Adonis, we should do pretty well," Lance replied.

Lance was the owner and CEO of Get Right Records, a new independent record label. He hired Adonis to do some artist development for him.

"I got some big plans for your artists. Don't forget we have a studio appointment next week, so Rome can drop a verse for your artists," Adonis said.

"How could I forget that?" Lance said.

Fat Tommy changed the subject. "You heard about that new Hip Hop police unit they came out with to profile rappers in NYC?" Tommy asked.

"Yeah, I was reading something about it. I don't see them targeting Rock n' Roll artists or Country artists. They see young successful Black millionaires and they have to fuck with us," Rome said.

"When are they ever going to stop the bullshit and just let us live? Every time a rapper does anything wrong, he is put on front page. How come they don't do that when we open up community centers, or donate to inner city schools? All they do is focus on the little bad and pay no attention to the greater good of rap music. Rap music sells more records than any genre. It brings a multitude of races and ethnic groups together. That's a beautiful thing. That's what they should be focusing on," Fat Tommy said.

All four men shook their heads in agreement to Fat Tommy's statement. "We can't let their evil deeds stop us from elevating this art form to its peak. It's already the top selling genre in the country. I remember when the major labels wanted nothing to do with Hip Hop. As soon as they seen that there was money in it they hopped on the band wagon. Not only did we become a multi-billion dollar industry, but we are the dominant culture. Now you can see all these commercials with rap jingles in them. As soon as they put rappers in their ads, they double their profit margin. Now all the major corporations have figured out that Rap equals profit," Fat Tommy said. He was a veteran in the industry.

"I remember when no one even wanted a Black person in their ads or our 'Jungle Music'," Lance said imitating a white man's voice.

"Now all of them have jungle fever. All the young white kids across America are listening to this jungle music. We work the hardest and get paid the least. Corporate America has its hands so deep in Hip Hop's pockets...Its ridiculous," Adonis said.

"That's how they always do it. We invent it and they either steal it or duplicate it and give it a new name. Then give us the scraps," Lance said.

"Hell, look at N'Sync and the Back Street Boys, and Britney Spears," Fat Tommy added.

"We are making more money than we ever did in the history of us being in America. We are still being robbed. Look at my label. When I was a small time guy selling 20,000 units here, 50,000 there, I wasn't a millionaire, but I was doing pretty well for myself. When I got on a major label for distribution, yeah, I got national exposure, but less money per unit. The advantage is that with them, I'll sell 200 to 300,000 units in blocks as opposed to the 20 to 50,000 I sold without a major. In the long run, I'll make a lot of money faster, but I'm still coming up shorter," Lance said.

"What we need is our own manufacturer, distribution and retail stores. With all of those three components in place, we'll have 100% ownership of everything. No money goes outside of our circle unless we want it to. Until then, we have to depend on the majors to distribute and manufacture our music," Adonis said with a nod of agreement from the other men.

The men were so engulfed in their conversation that they didn't notice their Queens were listening to them speak. They too nodded in agreement to Adonis' statement. Monica got a jolt of honorary pride because of the great dominance in his speech.

That's my king, Monica thought with a smile of royalty on her face

"We are too busy hating on one another and competing with each other. We have enough money to buy chains of retail stores and the manufacturing plants to press up the CD's and the trucks to distribute them. We already own the labels that produce the great music. Everyone will be multi-millionaires. But no, if I can't run it all I'm not making the next man rich. That is the attitude that most of our people have towards one another. That's why we will always get the scraps and work the hardest. How do you think the majors do it? Yeah, they compete, but not to the point where they're going to lose control of the whole pie," said Adonis

After a slight pause, Adonis continued. He said,"We have to get all of the big time Black record execs together: Russell Simmons, Jay-Z, Damon Dash, Jermaine Dupri, Master P, Ronald and Baby Williams. Every Black Man in the business who can make a difference needs to come together and devise a unified plan. THAT'S THE ONLY WAY WE CAN BECOME A MAJOR. IT'S TIME FOR THE BLACK MAN TO RISE AND TAKE HIS PLACE AT THE TABLE OF THE MASTERS."

Adonis spoke with so much fire that everyone in the room felt his heat. He tapped into everyone's mind within earshot of his words.

Monica was the first to clap. In unison, everyone else began to applaud him. Adonis stood proud and humble. He wasn't the type to gloat. His reward was him knowing that his words enlightened someone.

Monica stood next to her King like a proud Queen. She looked down at her new engagement ring and it was sparkling so much that she was captivated by its beauty. She looked up into Adonis's eyes, and then she kissed him on his lips.

"I love you, Adonis."

"I love you more my beautiful Black Queen."

They came to the party as lovers. They left as fiancés and soon-to-be Husband and Wife.

CHAPTER 15

Monica was a month past her due date. Any day now, she could go into labor. She couldn't wait to have this baby. Adonis was not only driving her crazy, he was driving himself crazy. If Monica got up to use the bathroom at night he would jump up out of his sleep, thinking it was time. Adonis would say, "I'm ready honey. Your bag is already packed. Breathe."

"I'm just using the bathroom, Adonis. It's not time yet," Monica answered each time.

"I was just making sure. Timing is everything."

"I know honey, and believe me, it will be soon."

One day Monica was at home by herself taking a shower. She felt pressure in her vagina when her water broke. Even with the water running, she knew what it was.

She was all alone and she was about to panic. Adonis went to work and there was no one there to take her to the hospital. She called an ambulance and then she called Adonis. Adonis wasn't in his office and he didn't have his cell phone on him. She left a message with the secretary.

The ambulance was there fairly quickly. When she got to the hospital, Adonis was already there. He had a nervous look on his face. He was so nervous that he was drenched from perspiration. Adonis looked like he was the one having a baby from the way he was worrying.

Monica was very relaxed. She was breathing the way she was taught. Adonis was a mess. He was swaying as if he was about to pass out.

"Sir, are you all right?" a passing doctor asked Adonis. "You look like you are about to faint. Maybe we need to look at you."

"No, I'm OK. My fiancé is in labor and I'm just a little nervous," Adonis replied.

"Oh, I see. Maybe you need to take a mild sedative to relax. Everything will be fine."

The words from the good doctor were sweet to the ear, but Adonis was still sweating.

After eight hours in labor, Monica gave birth to an eight pound baby boy. Monica was holding her new baby when the nurse came into the room holding a clip board. "Ms. Pernell we need to know what you are going to name your son."

"His name will be Adonis Ptah Nkosi, the Second."

The nurse wrote the name on the clipboard.

Adonis Jr. was a beautiful baby, just like Trina said he would be. He had dimples like his mother and a tuft of curly hair like his father. He was light skinned like his mother, but the tips of his ears indicated that he would get a little darker.

"I think I'll call him AJ, short for Adonis Jr."

"Sounds good to me," Adonis replied.

AJ came home two days later. Everything he needed was in his nursery. Adonis took a vacation from work to spend time with his new baby boy. That was good for Monica because it gave her some time to recover. Eight pounds was a lot of baby to come out of a twelve centimeter opening.

Adonis took care of everything from feeding AJ to changing his diaper. He even got up at 2 in the morning to tend to AJ. It wasn't a problem for Adonis. He enjoyed taking care of the little tyke.

AJ quickly became attached to his father. After a week, Monica began to do more for the baby. All baby boys have a natural attachment to their mothers. AJ's eyes lit up and he smiled whenever he saw Monica. When he would smile, it would brighten up his mother's whole soul. There was no joy to her like that of her new baby.

Trina and Rome came over to visit the new baby. They were on vacation in the Bahamas when Monica had AJ. They were just now coming back. When they left for their trip, Monica was due. When they returned, AJ was already a week old.

Trina was holding AJ and talking baby talk to him. AJ was a natural ladies man just like his father. He immediately became attached to all females. He smiled and cooed while Trina held him.

"Look at him. He is so fresh, trying to charm me with those dimples," Trina said.

"Let me hold him for a minute, Trina?" Rome asked.

Trina handed him over to Rome. AJ wiped the smile off his face and stared strangely at Rome.

"Yeah, he is going to be a ladies man all right. I can tell already. He is also going to be smart because Adonis is going to teach him his history early."

AJ was a happy little baby. He didn't cry all day like some babies. He only cried when he was wet or needed a bottle.

"I'm glad he isn't like Tavon was when he was a baby. Tavon would cry until he turned purple," Trina said.

"I'm glad, too because if I saw my little man turn purple, I'd go nuts."

Makeda came into the room. "Daddy, when can I start changing AJ's diaper?" Makeda asked.

"When Monica shows you how."

"Here, I'll show you. It's easy," said Monica. Makeda caught on quickly. She was a big help around the house. While Monica cleaned the house, Makeda would watch her little brother.

Monica was out of work for six months. She didn't plan on going back until AJ was at least a year old. Pamela from Fresh Faces told Monica she could return whenever she was ready. Monica was Fresh Faces most requested model, not only for the rap videos, but she was also a favorite for runway and print work.

She enjoyed staying at home and being a mom. She started working out to lose the pouch she gained during pregnancy. AJ would watch his mother jumping up and down every morning. He would laugh his little heart out. He thought that seeing his mother exercise was the funniest thing in the world.

AJ was starting to take on distinct features. When he was first born he didn't look like his mother nor Adonis. He had his own look. AJ began looking more and more like Adonis every day. He was going to be tall like Adonis because he had big hands and feet. He was going to be a big kid.

It's a funny thing watching babies grow up. They go through the different stages so fast, it's unbelievable. It's almost like blinking your eyes and they're walking. Turn around and they are in high school.

The cycle of life is a process of growth and development. There is no set amount of time when you are supposed to figure out your purpose in life. Some people live their whole life without finding out their purpose. Others find out eventually. Life is short. It happens so quickly and then you're gone.

AJ's first birthday party was like a toddler's extravaganza. His party was held at the same Discovery Zone where Adonis and Monica met 3 years ago. They hired a magician and AJ's favorite cartoon characters.

AJ was spoiled to death. He got attention from every corner of his existence. If his big sister wasn't spoiling him, his parents and his Grandparents, and Uncle Geno were spoiling him.

His grandparents were ecstatic over the little prince. They began coming out to Brooklyn every weekend to see their new grandson. Uncle Geno visited his nephew often as well.

Geno got his act together. He admitted himself into a drug program to combat his marijuana habit. He was taking his new job seriously.

Geno got his own apartment down the block from Adonis. He even had a steady girlfriend who worked as a stylist for Fresh Faces. Her name was Candy and she was a beautiful woman. She had a caramel complexion and long, black hair that complemented her slim face.

Everything in Adonis and Monica's world was perfect. They had a loving relationship, great careers and a beautiful family. There was nothing to complain about. Nevertheless, somehow destiny always has an uncanny way of disrupting paradise. Just when you thought it was safe, disaster strikes.

One day on his way from his office, Adonis was at a red light. When the light turned green, he pressed the gas. Out of nowhere, BAM! He was hit by a car running a red light, doing about 45 miles per hour.

The damage would not have been so bad if the car was hit on the passenger side. That wasn't the case. Adonis was hit on the drivers' side, knocking him into a coma. He suffered from major internal injuries to his kidneys, spleen and liver. Adonis was alive but it didn't look good for him. He was in critical condition.

When Adonis reached the hospital, the doctors didn't think he would make it. The damage to his body was so severe that the doctors thought he should have died on impact. The fact that he was still alive baffled them.

When Monica heard about the accident, she rushed to the hospital. She called Adonis' parents and told them what happened. She was panicking already and she had not even gotten to the hospital.

When she arrived at the hospital, the doctors informed her of the damage. It didn't sound good to her. "Is he going to live?" Monica asked.

The doctor's expression alone told her the answer. The thought of Adonis dying made her weak. She fell onto the floor and went in convulsions.

"We need help over here!" The doctor yelled.

They got her to an emergency room and shot her with some drugs to stop the convulsions. Now both Monica and Adonis were in hospital rooms. The only difference was that Adonis' condition was critical.

When Adonis' parents got to the hospital, they were informed of his condition. They were also told about

Monica. Mrs. Nkosi dropped her head and shook it from side to side.

"Lord, please," she said in a soft whisper.

"Is my son going to live?" Mr. Nkosi asked.

The doctor gave them the same look that he gave Monica. "It doesn't look good right now. We cannot operate on the internal damage. We stopped the bleeding, but the organs have to heal on their own," Dr. Duverney, the doctor in charge, said.

"Will they heal, considering the damage?" inquired Mrs. Nkosi.

"It is too early to tell right now. The only problem concerning the damage to the organs is that we cannot chance going in and operating. He could die from system failure before they get a chance to heal. Then there is the coma situation. Right now, all we can do is hope for the best." Dr. Duverney walked away from them after his last statement.

Monica didn't wake up until 3 hours later. She almost forgot what happened. Then it all came back to her like a nightmare. She stepped slowly off of the bed. She was dizzy when she took her first step. A nurse came into the room.

"Ms. Pernell, please lay down. The sedative we gave you hasn't worn off yet," the nurse warned.

"I have to see my King," Monica demanded in a half cry. "Just let me see him please!"

The nurse agreed. She escorted Monica down the hall to his room. Adonis was hooked up to all kinds of tubes and machines. Just the sight of seeing her King like this made her cry so hard she couldn't see clearly.

161

"Please don't die, baby. I need you. The kids need you. I know you can hear me." Monica pleaded with him. "We need you, please don't leave us."

Monica spoke from the essence of her soul. She spoke as if her words alone would make him all right, but they didn't. Adonis had one foot in the grave. Only time would tell the outcome.

She sat at the side of his bed all night without any sleep. She stared at him, hoping to see some sign of life enter his body; a twitch of a finger or an eyelid, anything. All night there was nothing that indicated that Adonis was going to live. Adonis lied there as if he was dead. The machines were breathing for him.

Monica began to think about all the times that they shared together. How thoughtful, caring and considerate Adonis was. How knowledgeable he was. Just yesterday she kissed him off to work, a happy family man so full of life. A day later, he was lying there with no life in him.

There was still hope for Adonis. The doctors didn't give him 24 hours to live, but he was still alive. Everything depended on how fast his body could heal itself, so his organs could function properly. If his organs healed enough to function, then he had a 90% chance of living.

Then there was the coma situation. The thing about comas was there was no telling when a person would come out of one. It could take weeks, months, sometimes even years before someone recovered from one. People have been known to be in a coma for 20 years and then suddenly come out of it.

Monica was at the hospital for 48 hours straight with only four hours of sleep. Her body was exhausted

162

but her mind wouldn't let her rest peacefully. She had to tend to AJ and Makeda. They told Makeda that her father was in a car accident. She went into a deep depression. Makeda was fearful whenever she heard about car accidents because her mother died in one. She was old enough to understand life and death. Now she was worried that her father was going to die because of a car accident, just like her mother.

"If he is going to be all right, why isn't he home with us?" Makeda asked Monica. Monica just looked at her. "You're just telling me he is going to live. He is going to die just like my mother."

Makeda ran to her room in tears.

AJ didn't know what was going on. All he knew is that his hero wasn't home. He got used to being with his father every day. AJ missed him.

"Ma-ma, Da-da." That was his way of asking for his father.

"He'll be here soon, baby." That's all Monica would tell him.

It had been a week since the accident. He was still in the coma, but there was good news. The doctors said that his organs were functioning correctly. He was making a major recovery in that area. That meant that he wouldn't die from system failure. There was still the coma issue he had to deal with.

"Your fiancé must have been a strict vegetarian. We notice that vegetarians have stronger organs because they do not strain their organs. The body strains to digest meat, but it digest vegetables with ease. So vegans' organs are much stronger than meat eaters."

"Yes, he is a strict vegetarian. He hasn't eaten any meat in over ten years."

That bit of news made Monica feel better. She had faith in her King's strength. She spoke to him every day by his side. She knew that he could hear her. The doctors urged her to talk to him.

"That's right baby. Fight. Don't let death win, not yet. You have so much more work to do. I know you are going to make it," said Monica as she attempted to convince herself to believe her own words.

She held his hands while she spoke to him. He was still non-responsive.

"Come back to me, baby. I love you." She kissed him gently on the lips. "I love you more, Adonis." Just then something happened. His finger moved. She felt it. The movement shocked her. She yelled out for the doctor with excitement.

"Dr. Duverney! His finger moved!" She screamed into the intercom.

"What happened, Ms. Pernell?" Dr. Duverney asked.

"I was talking to him and I kissed him and then his finger moved."

"It could have been an involuntary movement, a muscle spasm. Let's go see, just keep talking to him."

Monica spoke to him. She kissed him and talked some more. Nothing happened; no movement.

"Like I said Ms. Pernell it was probably a muscle spasm." The doctor left the room.

Monica stayed in the room all night. She fell into a deep sleep. She was having a dream of her and Adonis in a field of daisies, playing with each other. They were laughing and having the fun that lovers have. Adonis embraced Monica and kissed her. They fell on top of the daises.

"I told you that I love you more," Adonis said to her in the dream.

She shook her head, no.

"No, you don't. I love you more."

"Remember, I'm the originator of loving more." He kissed her passionately and then she woke up. The dream seemed so real to Monica. It was one of those intense dreams. She was recalling all of the images in the dream trying to figure out the significance of them. She thought about everything that happened step by step.

"He told me that he loves me more in the dream." She spoke out loud to herself. Then a thought hit her like a sledge hammer. "That's it. That's what I said to him earlier when he moved his finger. I love you more then he moved his finger."

She walked over to him and bent down to speak directly into his ears. The only light in the room illuminated from a night light over his head board. She held his hand and kissed him. She took a deep breath and she spoke from the depths of her soul. "I love you more, Adonis."

The words sparked something in his lifeless body because he moved his finger again. The slight movement almost scared Monica to death this time. She gasped for a quick gulp of air.

"Adonis baby, I love you so much more. Please wake up baby."

This time his eyes fluttered as if he wanted to wake up from a nightmare. She was so excited by now that she just spoke a jumbled up sentence loudly into his ear.

"Adonis, baby, I love you more. Come on baby, get up. I love you more than anything in this world. "

With every word she spoke, his finger moved and his eyes fluttered more.

"Come on Adonis, you can do it. Do it for me. Do it for Makeda. Do it for Adonis Jr."

When she spoke of Makeda and Adonis Jr., she saw the whites of his eyes start to show.

"Adonis Jr. loves you more, too, and so does Makeda."

Finally, he opened his eyes. He was incoherent to everything around him. Nevertheless, he was awake from the coma. He didn't move his body. He didn't even focus on anything. He just lied there with his eyes open.

Monica pressed the button for the night doctor to come to the room. He was there within 20 seconds.

"What's wrong, Miss?" The doctor asked.

With tears in her eyes and joy in her heart, she spoke. "He is alive. My King is alive."

The doctor moved quickly into action.

"We need to keep him stable." The doctor called for a nurse and she was there in a flash to assist him. The doctor shined a small light into Adonis' pupils. He responded by squinting.

"That's a good sign. Mr. Nkosi, if you can hear me, all I want you to do is nod your head yes."

It took Adonis some time to register, but he slowly nodded yes. Monica was about to scream from the excitement she was feeling.

166

It took about an hour before Adonis was totally coherent. He had temporary amnesia. He couldn't remember his name or who Monica was for about 5 days. With some psychiatric therapy, his memory came back. He slowly remembered everyone in his family.

Adonis stayed in the hospital for a month after he came out of his coma. He went from 225 lbs. to 190 lbs. in the short time he was hospitalized. He looked skinny, but Monica didn't care. All that mattered to her was that her king was alive and well. He had to wear a neck brace and he walked with a cane. Other than that, he was OK.

His first day home from the hospital was a joyous occasion. Everyone was at his brownstone to greet him. When he walked through the front door, Makeda yelled, "Daddy!" She ran to him and hugged his waist.

"Da-da! Da-da!" AJ yelled while running in circles.

Adonis strained to bend over and pick him up.

"Take it easy, baby. You heard what the doctor said. Nothing strenuous for at least 3 months," Monica instructed.

"It would've been more strenuous for me *not* to pick him up," Adonis replied.

Geno was sitting on the couch with his new girlfriend. He stood up to greet his big brother with a handshake and a manly hug. "Good to see you big brother. Shit has been hectic down at the office. I've been holding it down," Geno said like a true vet.

"Thank you, Geno. I knew you could do it. You just needed to focus. I'm proud of you."

Rome and Trina had approached him and gave him their love. His parents were there to greet him as well.

Monica was his caretaker and she was going to see to it that he followed the doctor's orders.

"OK everyone; this is his first day home. The doctor said that he will need lots of rest and relaxation," said Monica.

Adonis went to his room to lie down and watch TV for the rest of the day.

Monica walked in the room and watched Adonis while he watched TV.

"It's good to have you back my King."

"It's good to be back, my Queen." They kissed.

It was Monica's turn to wait on Adonis hand and foot like he did when she was pregnant. She had no problem with it. She was happy to tend to him. With all the love Adonis received, it boosted his spirits which helped him recover. He was enjoying life again.

One day Monica was thinking about the night that Adonis came out of the coma. She never discussed the whole event with him in detail. "You know I love you more, right Adonis?" Monica asked.

"Yes sweetheart, I know."

"Seriously, when you were in that coma, I told you I love you more. The first time your fingers twitched. Then later on that night I fell asleep and I had a deep dream. In the dream you were telling me that you love me more and then I said it to you. Then you told me to remember that you were the originator of loving more and I woke up."

Adonis had a look of deep thought as his Queen spoke.

"I was trying to interpret the dream when it hit me. The words *I love you more* caused you to respond. I leaned to your ear and spoke from the bottom of my heart. I told you that I love you more. Then I told you that AJ and Makeda love you more. Your fingers twitched, and then your eyes opened."

Adonis listened to the story like he remembered the dream himself. He recalled hearing the words spoken in his ear. It was as if it was in a dream. He had a strange feeling that he could remember everything she said. He sat silently for a few minutes, trying to figure it out. He had a look of confusion on his face.

"What are you thinking about honey?"

"I was just having a recall of those words. For some reason, it felt like a dream when I try to imagine it."

Adonis was still in deep thought. He looked at Monica and spoke to her like the philosopher he is. "Maybe, life is nothing but a dream. When you wake up, you're dead."

"Maybe you're right."

CHAPTER 16

It took Adonis almost a year before he fully recovered. He had developed a phobia for driving. Whenever he heard a loud, crashing noise, he had flash backs of the accident. He also suffered from migraine headaches. Other than that, he was happy to be alive.

Adonis and Monica decided to hold off on the wedding until he recovered. Now that he felt better, it was time to tie the knot. They had disagreements about the preparations for the wedding. Monica wanted a large wedding and Adonis wanted a small one. To Adonis, it was less of a headache to have a simple, modest wedding. He also thought about the cost of having a large wedding.

For Monica, it was like a fairytale come true. Her reasons for wanting a large wedding had more to do with her childhood. When she was young, she always dreamed about meeting her Prince Charming. Well, Adonis was her Prince Charming. She wanted to throw a huge ceremony to celebrate her dream come true.

"I don't see the need in having a big wedding, to spend thousands entertaining phony people who really don't wish us well. As soon as something goes wrong in our marriage, they will be the first to talk bad about it. I'd rather entertain the few friends and family we have. At least they will try to console us if we have any problems."

"You keep saying we are going to have problems. Is there something I should know about before we get married?" asked Monica in a slightly worried tone.

"No, I don't plan on having any problems. I hope we *never* have any problems. I was just generally speaking. Things happen you know."

"Well I still want to have a big wedding. Ever since I was a little girl I dreamed of meeting my Knight in shining armor. Now that I found you, I want my fairytale wedding to come with you."

Adonis looked into Monica's eyes and he couldn't deny her. He understood her reasons for wanting a big wedding now. "Anything, for my Queen." Adonis kissed her on her forehead. "On one condition."

"Anything, just tell me," said Monica.

"You will be in charge of getting everything together. I don't want the headache. I'm going to give you a budget. If you exceed the budget, then you are paying the extra out of your own pocket. Deal?"

"Deal. I love you more." She kissed him on the lips sealing their deal.

Monica turned her wedding plans into a campaign. Every day for a month she called caterers, wedding halls, wedding gown makers, limousine companies, florists and travel agencies.

She got advice from Karen, one of her model friends from Fresh Faces. Karen married a multi-millionaire a year ago. Monica knew that with a budget of $150,000 she couldn't possibly match Karen's wedding. She was just getting advice from her.

Monica finally narrowed her choices down to what she could afford. She began making appointments and getting the dates secured. They were going to entertain anywhere from 200 to 300 people. As a gift, an artist that

Adonis managed would sing one of her hit love songs from her new album.

The wedding day was only two days away. Everything was in place. Monica did a good job of taking care of all the details. Now, all that was left was for them to tie the knot. Monica was anxious like a kid on Christmas morning.

Adonis was just as anxious as Monica He was nervous about getting married again. He was never one to be the center of attention. He knew what it would be like at the wedding with all eyes on him. He felt the same way when he married Tammy. That's why they had a small gathering at his first wedding.

A day before the wedding, Rome had a surprise bachelor party set up for Adonis. He had to keep it a secret because he knew how Adonis felt about strippers. Rome thought, how could he object to something that he knew nothing about? Rome was a traditionalist. In his eyes, every man should have a bachelor party.

Rome set everything up perfectly. He rented a suite at the Hyatt. He told Adonis that it was a private listening party for a new artist. When they entered the suite, all of Rome and Adonis's friends yelled out, "Surprise!"

Adonis was definitely surprised.

"Hey man I had to do it to you this way. I knew you were not going to let me throw you a bachelor party," Rome said.

Adonis was about to object, but he decided against it. Besides, all of their friends were there.

"You got me this time. You sly dog you." Adonis playfully tapped Rome on his chin.

They had cases of champagne and there was food on the table. Music played on a system provided by the hotel. Rome knew Adonis would loosen up after he had a few drinks. By the time the real entertainment arrived, he would be nice and tipsy.

"Come on Adonis, have a few drinks. Hey man, it's your bachelor party. Loosen up. I'm driving, so you don't have to worry. Just chill," Rome instructed.

Adonis took the glass and drank. He thought it tasted sweet. "This stuff isn't bad. I think I'll have another one." Adonis ended up drinking almost the whole bottle. He was feeling very tipsy, not drunk.

There was a knock on the door. "Who is it?" Rome asked. He knew exactly who it was.

"Someone called for room service?" the voice on the other side inquired.

"Oh yeah, I forgot I called them almost 20 minutes ago," Rome pretended.

He opened the door and two beautiful, thick Black women pushed in a long table that was covered. They wore maid uniforms.

"We thought you fellas could use a little live entertainment," one of the women said in a sultry tone.

Then Sisqo's famous stripper anthem blasted out of the speakers. *"Let me see that thong! That thong th-thong thong thong."* Two more women came out from under the table.

There were four strippers all together. Cinnamon, Chocolate, Vanilla and Strawberry. Strawberry was the thickest and most gorgeous of the four. She had on a strawberry shaped thong covering her crotch. Strawberry had the body of a goddess. Her face was sweet and

173

innocent like an angel. Her complexion was a smooth light brown.

The four women began to shake their tits and asses all over the place. Adonis was now so intoxicated that he didn't object. In fact, he joined in the fun.

"Who is the man of the hour?" Strawberry asked.

Everyone pointed to Adonis. Strawberry seductively walked over to him. Adonis was mesmerized by this woman.

"You are fine. Too bad you are getting married. We could have a lot of fun together."

She sat Adonis down in a chair and all four women gathered around him. They gave him an exclusive show. Adonis was feeling the moment. He continued to drink, which made him loosen up even more. The women drank also. Everyone was practically drunk.

Then two of the women took Adonis in a room and closed the door. That was the last that anyone saw of Adonis.

When Adonis woke up the next day, he had a vicious hangover. He looked down and noticed he was naked. Then he looked to both sides and there were two women on both sides of him. They were naked, too.

"What the hell is going on? Where are my clothes?" Adonis asked. He closed his eyes to try to remember what happened. It started to come back to him.

"Oh no, I didn't. I couldn't have."

"Yes, you did, and it was good. Your wife is a lucky woman," Strawberry answered.

"What time is it?" He looked at his watch. It was 11 am. The wedding was at 1 pm.

He got up, put on his clothes, and went to the bathroom. He looked in the mirror and he couldn't believe his eyes. He had hickies all over his neck.

"Oh my god, I can't believe this shit. Monica is going to kill me."

There was no way to hide the hickies all over his neck. They were all over his chest too. He was at a loss for words at the sight of the big red marks on his body. He could hide the ones on his chest, but not the ones on his neck.

"I'm in big trouble, fucking with Rome. No, I can't blame him, I'm a grown man. I just have to face the music."

Adonis left the room and went out into the large room and saw everyone laid out all over the suite. He found Rome.

"Rome, come on man get up!" Rome slowly got up. He had a hangover, too. Rome took one look at Adonis and saw his neck.

"Oh shit! What the fuck happened to you? Damn Adonis!" Rome couldn't believe his eyes.

"Come on we have to go get ready for the wedding."

They got everyone up and they all left the suite together. It was time to get ready for the big day.

One thing was good for Adonis. By tradition it was bad luck for the groom to see the bride before the wedding. When she did see the marks, he could tell her the truth and she would understand, or so he hoped.

Everything was in place. The wedding hall she selected was huge. Everything was luxurious. Adonis was at the groom's post looking as nervous as ever. People

175

couldn't help but see all of the hickies on his neck. Adonis felt like a spectacle.

The traditional "Here Comes the Bride" song began to play. Cameras flashed like a thousand sparks of light. People were in awe at the sight of the beautiful woman walking down the aisle.

"She's beautiful." People whispered comments about Monica's looks as she passed them.

Monica was being escorted by Mr. Townsend, Trina's father. He was more like a father to Monica than her own father had ever been.

Adonis didn't even want to turn his head to see her coming. When she finally reached the alter, he turned his marked up neck towards her. She was a vision of loveliness. She hadn't looked so beautiful to him in all of their time spent together. Today, she was the most incredible beauty he had ever seen. He kept eye contact with her. She didn't look at his neck. She stared into his eyes.

The pastor did the honors of bonding the ceremony. They went through all of the traditional exchanging of the vows and the rings, and then the kiss, which sealed everything. Through it all, Monica didn't pay attention to Adonis' neck even once.

After the wedding there was a reception. That was when Monica noticed Adonis's neck for the first time. At first she didn't know what it was. Then she looked closer.

"What the fuck happened to your neck?" Monica asked.

Trina saw the marks and she wondered when Monica would see them. Trina didn't want to be the bearer of bad news.

"Listen baby, let me explain. Let's go over there in the corner so we can have some privacy."

They strolled over to the corner like nothing strange was going on. Trina and Rome watched from their table. They knew what was going on.

"Last night, Rome threw me a surprise bachelor party. I didn't know anything about it until I got there. I started drinking and you know I can't hold my alcohol. Rome hired these strippers to entertain us. All I know is that I woke up with hickies on my neck." Adonis looked at her with puppy dog eyes. She knew he was telling the truth.

"I can't believe you. A day before our wedding and you pull this shit. That's why you were saying all that shit about us having problems. We haven't been married 24 hours and we are having problems, just like you said."

"You know I would never do anything intentionally to jeopardize our wedding or our relationship. It was an honest mistake. Please forgive me. Let's go back to the party and have a good time."

"OK, you're right. Why waste all of this money and not enjoy it."

"I love you more my Queen." Adonis kissed her face.

"I love you more, too." *But boy do I have a trick for your ass. A nice trick, Monica thought.*

After the wedding reception, they had plans to honeymoon for two weeks. First they would catch a flight to the Cayman Islands. From there, they would go on a cruise to Aruba, and then back to the U.S. Before they boarded the plane, Monica stopped at a store to get a few things.

177

"Stay here. I don't want you to see what I'm getting. It's a surprise," said Monica.

After she went to the gift shop, they boarded the plane headed for the Cayman Islands. While they were on the plane, Adonis fell asleep. Monica looked at him and she saw the red marks on his neck. She smiled because of the thought she had. She couldn't hold back the devious smile that was on her face.

After about six hours, they finally reached their destination. They had a deluxe honeymoon suite at one of the exclusive hotels on the island. The island they were on was beautiful. It had pure white sand and clear blue water. All of the beauty of the Caribbean was there on that island.

It was morning when they arrived. They slept on the plane, so they weren't tired. They showered and got dressed. They ate at a restaurant downstairs in the hotel. After they ate, they went on a tour of the whole island. The entire island was breathtaking. There was a string of islands all disconnected by a short stretch of clear blue water.

After touring all day, they were exhausted. They retired to their suite fairly early. When they got back to the suite, Monica slipped into an elegant Victoria Secret gown. She looked very enticing in it. It came just past her crotch, showing off her smooth, thick legs.

"Come here. You are the most beautiful woman in the universe," Adonis said in his most sexy tone.

"Whoa, not so fast tiger. I have a surprise for you; something really special." She walked over to her suitcase and pulled out a blindfold.

"What's this?" Adonis asked.

178

"Its' a little game I want to play. Just go along with it. Don't spoil the fun."

Adonis allowed her to blindfold him. "This feels kinky."

There was a round light fixture bolted to the wall.

"Perfect," she said.

She pulled out a pair of handcuffs from her suitcase. She put the cuffs through the fixture and stood Adonis up and guided him to the fixture. "Put your hands up. Yeah, right there."

She put the cuffs on his wrist. Adonis moved his hands in protest of being cuffed.

"What is this Monica?" he asked. "You're handcuffing me? Come on now."

"Just play along with me. It's just a game, honey. We never play and it's our honeymoon."

"OK."

"There now, be a good boy." She caressed his penis. She licked his neck and his chest and then took his shorts off. He was butt naked. Monica kissed his penis.

"You like that, don't you?"

"Yes, do it some more," said Adonis in a low, sexy voice.

"Not so fast. There is more to come."

She went back to her suitcase and got out her whip, the same kind she used on Timothy, the banker. He was in for a big surprise.

"You ready honey?"

"Yes, I'm ready baby. Bring it to poppa."

She smiled deviously and then she cracked the whip hard on his bare ass cheeks.

"Oh shit!" he yelled out. "What the fuck are you doing? Monica, take these damn cuffs off of me now!" he demanded.

"Whopish!" she cracked the whip again on his ass. This time she made him jump.

"Owww! Come on now! Un-cuff me! I'm not playing anymore!" Adonis demanded to be un-cuffed again.

"Oh yeah, this game is over when I say it's over." She hit him with the whip two more times. "First of all, let's get one thing straight. You are in no position to be demanding anything. Second of all, when you speak to me, call me Massa. Is that understood?"

"You can't be serious Monica."

"Whopish!" The whip hit him harder this time.

"Massa!" He yelled out.

"That's better. You have been a bad slave. I'll teach you to go get drunk and let some." She hit him again. "Let some hussies put hickies on your neck!" She hit him again. "On the night before our wedding!" Then one more hit.

"I'm sorry. It will never happen again. Please Monica," Adonis pleaded.

"Whopish!" She hit him again.

"Sorry who?"

"Sorry Massa."

"Now we have a good understanding."

She walked over to him and rubbed his raw ass cheeks. They were burgundy red. He whimpered when she touched it.

"Does it hurt?" She asked with mock compassion.

"Yes Massa, it hurts. Now please un-cuff me."

"Good, because that pain can never equal the pain I felt when I saw those hickies on your neck on our wedding day."

"I get the point. Now could you please take the cuffs off? Please Massa."

"I don't know. You might try to hurt me. You promise that you want do anything to me?"

"I promise Massa."

"OK, you promise," said Monica. She went into her suitcase to get the cuff key. She looked in the spot where she thought she had put them. The cuff key wasn't there. She looked everywhere for them but she couldn't find them. Then she realized that she didn't bring the key. She began to panic thinking of a way to get the cuffs off of Adonis.

"What's taking you so long? These cuffs are starting to hurt my wrist."

"Hold on honey. I'm looking for the key."

She knew there wasn't any key. She looked around the room trying to find something to jimmy the cuffs open. She couldn't find anything.

"Umm, sweetheart, we have a small problem."

"Tell me after you take these cuffs off."

"That's the problem, honey. I can't find the key."

"You can't find the key? Please don't tell me that Massa. I mean, Monica."

"I wasn't thinking of that when I cuffed you. I was so anxious to punish you for those hickies that I forgot the key. I'm so sorry." She paused and thought about a solution. "I'll have to call room service and see if they can help us."

"Room service! What are you going to tell them? That you cuffed me to a wall blindfolded me and whipped me while I called you Massa?"

"What do you suggest?" asked Monica.

"Take this damn blindfold off of me and put my boxer shorts on," Adonis said with humiliation in his voice.

Monica called room service and told them about the problem. When they stopped laughing, they called the hotel security and they came up to the room to un-cuff Adonis.

When the hotel security left, the embarrassment left with them. The couple could not help but laugh about the situation. They were thinking about what the hotel staff must be thinking about them.

"I'm sorry for cuffing you without a key. That was real crazy of me. I was thinking about punishing you."

"And I'm sorry for getting drunk and allowing something like that to happen."

"So we are even?" she asked.

"Yes, we are even. I love your crazy ass. I can't believe you had me calling you Massa."

"I love you more my King."

The newlyweds embraced and made love that night like never before.

CHAPTER 17

The rest of their honeymoon was like paradise. The cruise was the most romantic adventure they ever had in their lives. Aruba was just as beautiful as the Cayman Islands. They dreaded the trip back to New York. They had such a nice time that neither wanted to come back.

"We should just pack all of our things and get the kids and move to Aruba," Monica suggested playfully. "It is so peaceful here. It seems so distant from the rest of the world."

"It is definitely no New York. That's for sure. This is like heaven compared to that hell hole."

All good things come to an end. AJ was getting aggravated over the absence of his parents. He was two now so he understood lots more. He was talking more now, "Where are my Mommy and Daddy?" AJ Asked

"They are on their honeymoon. They'll be back soon," Trina said as she hugged AJ. No matter how many times she answered that question, AJ still asked it 100 times a day.

When Monica and Adonis finally made it home, the children were ecstatic. Makeda was older so she wasn't as excited as AJ. AJ was so excited that he was running in circles.

"Mommy! Daddy!" AJ yelled at the top of his little lungs.

"Hi, baby! Mommy missed you too." Monica picked him up and kissed him. She could hardly hold him. He was getting big so fast.

Adonis hugged Makeda and then he grabbed his son from his mother's arms.

Monica and Adonis brought back souvenirs for everyone. Monica and Trina sat in the living room talking their usual girl talk while Adonis and Rome spoke about their business.

"Girl, you are not going to believe what happened on our first night on The Cayman Islands." Monica paused to make sure the kids weren't listening. "I decided to punish Adonis for the hickies on his neck. So I brought some handcuffs and a whip and I blindfolded him. I cuffed him to a wall with his back to me. I got him naked and then I whipped his ass. I made him call me Massa while I whipped him." The two women were laughing hysterically.

"You whipped him like you use to whip that white man?" Trina asked.

"Exactly like I used to do to his ass. But then he begged me to un-cuff him. I felt like he had enough punishment so I went to un-cuff him and I couldn't find the cuff key. We had to call room service to help us get the cuffs off. Fortunately for us, the hotel security had cuff keys."

Trina laughed so hard that Adonis and Rome looked in her direction. Adonis had a feeling about what was so funny. It had to be the handcuff caper, he thought to himself.

"Things have been a little hectic since you left for your honeymoon. Geno has been running things in the office," Rome said.

"That's good to hear. What seems to be the problem?" asked Adonis.

"It seems that Artist Records is having some internal problems. They are at a standstill on some issues. From what Fat Tommy told me, the owners and the members of the board are talking about selling the label. My new album could be affected," Rome said.

"This is not good. I remember the last time something like this happened with Grace's label and it killed her career. Let's just hope that they resolve whatever it is before it directly affects your sales."

"Yeah, let's hope so. I would have sold more albums than I already have by now."

"I'll call them up and see if I can't be of some assistance."

It was back to the grind for Adonis. He had relaxed and had fun in paradise for two weeks. Now two weeks felt more like two days. It is strange how time flies when you're having fun.

It was the total opposite for Monica. She had not gotten any new assignments since she had the baby. Pamela from Fresh Faces told her that she would have some work for her when she came back from the honeymoon. It seems that the Rap Video Queen wasn't in demand anymore. In fact, she wasn't the Queen any longer. The crown had gone to a younger, new model who was getting all of the work in the new videos.

Monica was no longer a hot commodity on the video scene or the runway or pictorial scenes. Maybe it was because of the extra width in her hips. She lost all of the excess weight that she put on during the pregnancy. But her hips seemed to spread out more. There was no hiding it.

To Adonis and any other Black Man, Monica had a beautiful shape. However, in the predominantly White world of modeling, those broad hips were not accepted.

Monica knew that her hips were the reason for not getting any work with the agency. She fell into a depression. Not because she couldn't get any work in modeling, but because she thought about what she could do besides modeling. The answer scared her. The only thing she knew how to do besides modeling was stripping.

Monica was 29 years old with no trade and no college education. She was good at modeling, but the way things looked, her modeling career was over.

Monica started to develop a low self-esteem. She never felt this way about herself. The thought that she had no job skills that caused her to feel this way. She looked in the mirror and questioned her beauty. She would ask herself questions in her mind every day. *Am I getting old? Am I fat? Am I still enticing as I was 3 years ago?*

She accepted the role as a housewife, taking care of her husband and the kids. However, she had a fire in her to do and become something else. For now, she settled for being a housewife.

Monica wanted to be something more than just a housewife, but she didn't know what it was yet. Every day, the fire in her was being distinguished little by little. The more she got into the routine of being a housewife, the more she accepted it. The more she accepted being a housewife, the more depressed she became. She was not content with just being a housewife.

Most women in her position would have been happy with how Monica lived. Monica was not most women. When Monica was younger, she always daydreamed that her future was a bright one. She didn't dream of being a stripper. She wanted to be a lawyer or a doctor. Even though she became a stripper, she was highly successful at it.

Monica has always been an over-achiever. Now she felt like she was changing into something she didn't like.

One day she asked Adonis some questions. She didn't want to approach him about her thoughts for fear that he would mistake her intentions. She wanted his opinion, but she didn't know how to go about getting it without exposing her feelings.

"Adonis, am I getting fat?"

He turned her around and raised his eyebrows at the sight of her voluptuous ass and hips.

"You are fat in all the right places. If you didn't have a little fat back there, it wouldn't be right," he replied half-jokingly.

"I'm serious, am I still as attractive to you now as I was when you first met me?"

"Of course you are honey. It seems like you get better with time. Come here, Queen." He hugged her and she cuddled up in his embrace.

"You always say the right things to make me feel better. I love you more. Thank you for being you."

"Don't mention it." He reminded her of their old saying *I love you more.*

That moment added a little fuel to her dwindling fire. However, a week later she was back in Depress-Ville again. She wanted a job. She was tired of being a housewife. There was no promising career in it. She felt useless just being a housewife. She missed the thrill of making her own money, lots of money.

She started looking in the newspaper every morning in the wanted ads. She circled jobs that she thought she could do. Things like customer service. She circled a few clerical jobs even though she couldn't type to save her life. She circled dance instructor, although she had no formal training. She could have been one, but exotic dancing doesn't count.

All of her choices narrowed down to customer service rep at Neiman Marcus. She called them up and set up an interview. She felt good just setting up the interview.

Her interview was scheduled for the next day. She got professionally dressed in a cream colored Gucci pantsuit. She looked very elegant. She looked the part of a Neiman Marcus customer service rep.

When she got to the interview, Monica noticed that she was the only African American in the whole store. This made her feel a little uncomfortable. Rich White folks have a way of making Black people feel uncomfortable without saying a word. They are quick to stereotype Blacks.

When it was Monica's turn to be interviewed, she went into the office and there was a White man sitting behind a desk.

"Hello, Mrs. Nkosi," he said in a friendly manner.

"Hello, Mr. Weinstein. How are you today?"

"I'm fine and you?"

"I could be better."

I could be better if I had this job, she thought to herself.

"That is a nice pantsuit you have on."

"Thank you, sir. I bought it here a few months ago."

Of course she was lying, but she knew they carried items like the one she had on. She marveled at how witty her comeback was. She had lots of practice lying when she was Banana Pudding. It had been four years since she was Banana Pudding.

The rest of the interview went fairly well. She could tell by the way Mr. Weinstein made comments that he was impressed by her charm. He told her that they would call her within the week and let her know if she got the job.

She felt like she accomplished something, even though it wasn't confirmed that she was hired. She called Trina to tell her the news. She had been confiding in her friend about how she was feeling, so Trina was abreast on everything.

"It looks good girl. I impressed him when he told me how nice my Gucci pantsuit was. I told him that I bought it in his store a few months ago."

"You were always quick with your game. That's that Banana Pudding in you," Trina responded.

"I was surprised how easily it flowed. I haven't done that in so long, but I guess some things always stay with you."

"So when will you know if you got the job."

"Hopefully I'll know this week." Monica heard a beep on the line indicating that she had an incoming call.

"Hello, may I speak to Monica Nkosi?" The caller asked.

"This is Monica speaking."

"Hello, Mrs. Nkosi, this is Martin Weinstein from Neiman Marcus. I called to tell you that you have the job as Customer Service Rep at Neiman Marcus. You can start Monday at 9am. Welcome aboard Mrs. Nkosi."

Monica was so happy to hear those words that she was quiet for a minute. What she didn't know was that Neiman Marcus had to meet a quota to hire minorities because they had none. They were being pressured to hire a minority, so Monica was their choice.

"Thank you so much for hiring me, Mr. Weinstein. I won't let you down."

"You are welcome. See you on Monday at 9a.m."

Monica clicked back over to Trina.

"Guess what girl! I got the job. That was Mr. Weinstein from Neiman Marcus."

"Congratulations. Damn that was fast! You just went for the interview today. I'm glad to hear that! Now you can stop being depressed around the house all day."

"I got to go. I'll talk to you later."

When Monday came, Monica was up at 6a.m. because she was so anxious to start work. They got AJ enrolled into a preschool day care center. His little life was about to change also. He was so used to being with his mother all day. It would take some time for him to get adjusted to being at a day care.

Adonis would take AJ to the day care center and Monica would take the subway to Manhattan to work. It was more convenient for her to take the train than to drive. The cost of parking would have cost her a fortune.

When Monica first arrived at Neiman Marcus that Monday morning, Mr. Weinstein introduced her to a skinny White woman named Kathy. Kathy was told to show Monica around and to give her the basic orientation of her every day duties.

Kathy was very arrogant towards Monica. She acted as though she didn't want the task of showing Monica around. She made it obvious that she didn't like Monica by the way she stopped to talk to her co-workers without introducing them to Monica.

Monica thought that was very rude, but she didn't blow her cool. She just went along with the scheme of things. It wasn't like being a Customer Service Rep was her lifelong goal. She didn't see it as some great lifetime achievement, just a job to get her out of the house.

She really didn't need orientation. She had done enough shopping to know what a Customer Service Rep does, which was simple to her. Help customers shop.

Her first day was dreadful. None of the women liked her. They didn't talk to her or eat lunch with her. They excluded her from their little club. Monica didn't really care. It was just that they created a difficult working atmosphere for her to adjust to.

When she was done with the first day, she knew it was going to be hard for her to adjust to her co-workers. Monica was not one to kiss anyone's ass.

"How was your first day at Neiman Marcus?" Adonis asked Monica.

"Terrible. All of the girls that work with me hate me. They are all White, everybody, even the customers."

"Don't worry, sweetheart. The first day is always the hardest day. They will start to like you. Who wouldn't like a magnetic person like you?" His words always seemed to uplift her spirits. She smiled.

"I don't know what I would do without you my King."

"Don't mention it." He winked his eye and kissed her forehead.

The next two days were the same as the first. It almost seemed as if it got worse. Whenever Monica would try to help a customer, one of the other girls would intervene.

"Excuse me miss, I'll help you with that. She is new."

They were trying to black ball her, trying to make it seem as if she was incompetent for the job. She found herself doing nothing, the same way she felt as a housewife.

This went on for the first week and then came the straw that broke the camel's back. Trina had come into the store to buy something. She was really there to see her friend at her new job. As she entered the store, Monica heard one of the girls say something derogatory about a Black woman. She didn't know that they were talking about Trina.

"There goes one of those Black bitches that steal. She's probably one of those what do they call them?"

"Boosters," Kathy replied.

Monica didn't see Trina enter the store so she wasn't aware they were speaking about Trina. She watched Kathy walk towards a Black woman. Monica had no idea that it was her best friend, Trina.

"Excuse me, but can I help you?" Kathy said in a disrespectful undertone.

Trina looked at her like she was crazy. She noticed the nasty tone she used to address her with.

"Did I ask you for any help?" she yelled at her.

"No but..."

"Then take your narrow ass somewhere and bother someone else."

"Why, I never!"

"Yes, you did. And you swallowed too."

It took Kathy a minute to figure out what Trina just said. When she did figure it out, she stormed off fuming mad.

Monica stepped to the area where Kathy spoke to the Black woman. When she saw that the woman who Kathy and her cohorts were harassing was Trina, Monica was furious. That was it. She took off her name plate and she was about to get *ghetto.*

Kathy and the other girls were in a huddle when Monica approached them. They became suddenly quiet when they saw Monica. They didn't want Monica to hear what they were saying.

"Let me tell you stank ass bitches something." She made sure she had their undivided attention. "You see that Black woman over there? Well, that is my sister and I heard and saw the whole encounter that just happened. She has never stolen anything in her life. She is more honest than any of you ugly bitches. You can have this dumb ass job! I quit! But not before I tell Mr. Weinstein how you treated my sister."

"Wait! We're sorry. You don't have to tell Mr. Weinstein," Kathy the ringleader said half pleading.

Monica noticed the change in her attitude when she mentioned telling Mr. Weinstein. She knew that she had something over her now. She was going to get her back for the past week that she treated her like shit. She was going to have some fun doing it.

"Oh no, he needs to know about this shit."

Monica walked towards Mr. Weinstein's office.

"Wait! Wait!" Kathy yelled as Monica got closer to the office.

Monica was smiling to herself at the way she turned the tables. She went into the office to tell Mr. Weinstein that she was quitting. She wasn't even going to tell him about the misconduct of his head Customer Service Rep. Then Kathy stormed into his office, all out of breath.

"Mr. Weinstein, I can explain. We just thought she was a woman who we previously caught stealing. That's why we approached her in that manner. It was an honest case of mistaken identity," Kathy spoke with a sorry look on her face.

"What the hell are you talking about Kathy?" Mr. Weinstein asked.

The most dumbfounded look appeared on Kathy's face. Monica wanted to laugh so bad at the spectacle she just made of herself. It was too late. She had to tell him what happened. When he heard what Kathy had done, he fired her on the spot.

This was not the first time Kathy had been involved with discrimination. It was the third incident. She had a history of displaying unjust behavior towards minorities.

On one occasion, the store almost got sued for Defamation of Character and Discrimination. Kathy did the same thing she did to Trina --to another Black woman--who happened to be the wife of the Comptroller of the City of New York.

Monica left her position. She felt like Customer Service Rep was not for her. Mr. Weinstein almost begged her to stay, but she stuck to her guns. She felt like she wasn't cut out for the job. She knew that she could do something else that was more meaningful to her.

Although Monica was back to point A; that is, being a housewife, she was determined to find something that she could do that would satisfy her appetite for success. She thought long and hard for the rest of that week about what she could do. She had a burning desire to be successful again like she was as Banana Pudding and the Rap Video Queen.

She spent every day thinking of things that she was really into, things she loved that would make her lots of money. Monica really enjoyed her short stint in modeling. However she knew that her career as a model was over.

Then one day as if by coincidence, she got an idea that changed her life. She and Adonis were talking about the modeling business. Adonis had made a good point about the predominantly White modeling industry.

"Since the Whites own everything, they set the standard of what and how people perceive beauty. Most super models are White, very slim, tall with no-ass-at-all. Except for a few Black token models that were fortunate enough to make it to the top." As usual, Adonis spoke with conviction.

You're right, all of the top paid models at Fresh Faces fit that very description," Monica replied.

195

"Someone should start an agency that caters to the Black market of models. There is definitely a large market for Black fashion. I mean Black people spend just as much money on clothing as any other ethnic group, possibly more. Why shouldn't there be more Black Models?"

Adonis sparked a thought in Monica. This was the idea that she was looking for. Something that she could get into that she enjoyed; something that she liked to do. Modeling was the only job that she had that she really enjoyed. The idea of starting a Black modeling agency was something she saw herself doing. She would be giving beautiful Black women a chance to start a career.

Adonis watched his wife stare into space as she thought about the possibilities of starting an all-Black modeling agency. Her wheels were turning 100 miles a minute. Adonis knew his wife very well. He knew when she had a good thought in mind, so he didn't interrupt her train of thought.

"That's it honey!" she said excitedly. "That's what I'm going to do. I'm going to start a modeling agency that caters to Black women."

Adonis thought about the idea. It was definitely up her alley because she was a successful model at one time. "I can help you get started with my contacts in the music industry. Music and fashion go hand in hand. That is a brilliant idea baby."

"*You* are brilliant. You are the one that sparked the idea. I'll call my agency Star Quality Modeling Agency so that everyone will know that I'm partners with Star Quality Artist Management," said Monica as she envisioned success with her new agency.

196

"Not a bad idea at all. It can help both of our businesses grow."

Monica wasted no time getting all the basic footwork done for her company. She got incorporated and got a license to run a modeling agency. She had to be registered with the Model Agency Guild. Once she got all of the groundwork accomplished, it was time to get some models.

She decided to run the agency from the Brownstone until she made enough money to rent office space. There was always a chance that her company would flop before it even got off the ground, so she could save money by running the company from the apartment.

She had a group of Black models that she became close friends with when she worked for Fresh Faces. Monica contacted them all and let them know that she had just started her own agency. She got instant support from all of her model friends. She told them that if they knew of any pretty Black women who wanted to be models and had a hard time finding an agency, they may contact her.

Monica even contacted some of her old stripper friends. There were a dozen or more gorgeous Black women that would make perfect models for her new agency. She had all of the models lined up to sign with her new agency. Now all she needed was the work.

She started contacting all of the Black clothing companies. Monica let them know that she was the new agency in town and that her agency was all Black women. At first, the Black designers were not quick to call her agency for models until she got her first big client.

Her first big client was a new Black-owned clothing company that was started by two brothers. The name of their clothing line was Thorough. They were blowing up everywhere. Their designs were trendy and fashionable for the inner city.

They called Monica because they heard about her agency through the grapevine. She still had people who remembered her from her Rap Video Queen days.

Thorough's spring women's line was hot. Monica got them the hottest females she had in her stable. All of her models were built like healthy Black women from the hood. They all had the popular big ass, some with big tits to match. Not fat, just voluptuous, firm bodied Black women.

The Thorough brothers were very pleased with the way the ads came out. The models that Monica sent them were exactly what they wanted. It was like a breath of fresh air to finally see gorgeous, well-built Black women on billboards and in magazines.

Thorough's spring line did so well from the models of Star Quality that they shot commercials advertising the models in their clothing. The commercial ads did so well that it almost doubled their sales.

Monica added Black male models to her roster as well. The men were the type of Black men that Black women preferred. Thorough used the male models from Star Quality for their men's line. Just like the success of the women's line, the men's line did well, too.

Monica's agency was the new talk of the town. Due to the success of Thorough using her agency for their line, every Black designer was calling Monica for models. After a while, even the major White clothing companies were calling for models. Within the first year of business, Monica had accounts with 15 clothing companies. As things picked up, it looked like she was going to double her clients in the second year.

Monica's agency was such a success that she had to rent out an office with enough space to accommodate the new staff of workers she had to hire. She wanted to rent out an office in an area that said, 'We mean business'. She wanted it to be in a prime location so that she could show the competition that she was a force to be reckoned with.

Monica chose to rent space in the Empire State Building. It was expensive, but she was already in the millions with the accounts she had. She had big accounts waiting to be closed. She wanted to make a statement to her new clients as well.

Monica was on the 45th floor. Her staff loved the fact that their new boss was this ambitious. Star Quality was so successful because it created a market that was already there. Minorities spend more money on clothes than any ethnic group. Yet we are the poorest group economically. WE don't own any major corporations, but we generate money for them as a working class of people. This fact was well-known by the major corporations. That's why they promote their products to minorities, draining our communities of our mighty spending power and giving nothing back.

Monica studied the dynamics of how economics worked in America. She began to understand that the major clothing companies knew that their urban lines grossed more money than the other lines. It all made sense to her why her company was doing so well. Use

Black models to promote to Black people. Simple mathematics in a nutshell. It didn't take a rocket scientist to figure it out.

In two years, Monica's Star Quality Modeling Agency grossed $50 million dollars. She cornered the market on the demand for Black models. She was the biggest all-Black modeling agency in the world. To say that she was successful was an understatement.

Monica and Adonis bought a large estate out in Long Island not far from Rome and Trina's estate. Her agency was doing so well that she had to lease the whole 45th floor. When she first rented the space on the 45th floor, she only had a small area. The business had come a long way.

Adonis also expanded his client list. He branched off into being a financial advisor for the models on Monica's roster. He was also their business manager. Five of the models in the agency were also music artist, who Adonis managed.

Star Quality was becoming a small conglomerate. They had plans to expand into sports and movie agents, as well as starting a record label and a movie production company; these would all be under the Star Quality umbrella.

It was amazing how their lives had changed almost overnight. Monica was going on her third year in business. Actually, Monica and Adonis were partners in all of their ventures. Adonis gave her the startup capital she needed to start her modeling agency. He was on paper as co-CEO of the modeling agency. She ran it, making her the founder and CEO.

There was never a disagreement between them concerning the business. Before success and the money, they had a strong foundation built on a mental connection and on love. A fortified relationship that neither money nor success could ever break. If they were to lose it all tomorrow, they would still have each other.

The money didn't change them; it changed their address and their bank accounts. They were still the same old Monica and Adonis. Perhaps that is a rare occurrence for people who attain their degree of success.

CHAPTER 18

The people around Adonis and Monica had a harder time adjusting to their success than they did. Everyone thought that the money should have changed them, so they approached them in a different manner. Their immediate family didn't approach them any differently. It was just their formal associates who did.

One day Adonis ran into Fat Tommy from Artist records. Adonis had not seen him in a year. He was delighted to see him. When Adonis greeted him, Fat Tommy sort of gave him the cold shoulder.

"What's popping Fat Tommy?" Adonis said to his longtime friend. He noticed that Tommy wasn't enthused to see him. "You act like you're not happy to see a brother."

"Oh, I'm supposed to be happy to see you? I guess because you're rich now, I'm supposed to be jumping for joy?"

Adonis was stunned at the way that Fat Tommy was acting. He would have never thought that he would act like that.

"That's what you think, that I think I'm better than you. Let me tell you something. I still put my pants on one leg at a time and my shit still stinks. Me and my wife work very hard to accomplish what we have. And we never look at ourselves as being better than anyone."

Fat Tommy thought about what Adonis just said. Maybe I came at him the wrong way. Adonis has always been a down to earth brother, Tommy thought.

"Pardon me Adonis for coming at you like that. I'm actually happy to see you man. I've just been going through some rough times. Artist Records is cutting back on their staff and I'm one of the people they're cutting back on. So I'm stressed right now."

"That's funny that I bumped into you because we are starting a record label. Rome is the President and we are looking for a Director of A&R department. Would you like the job?" asked Adonis.

"Of course, I need the work."

"Here is my number. Call the office tomorrow and we will go over everything from there. Welcome aboard my brother."

"Thank you, Adonis. Man I really needed this. And please, pardon me for the way I came at you."

Adonis stated, "Don't mention it. Just make sure you call me."

Incidents like that occurred frequently. Everyone that knew about their success expected something from them. Whether it was money or a certain attitude, people expected *something* from them.

They had become a bit famous for their achievements. Monica and Adonis were on the cover of Black Business Magazine and sometimes they made it in the tabloids. It was hard not to know who they were.

Geno practically ran the artist management company. Adonis gave him the Brownstone that he owned when they initially moved to Long Island. Geno and his girlfriend now lived there. Geno owned a brand new S550 Mercedes Benz that Adonis gave him as a birthday gift for stepping up his game. It was a bonus for all the work Geno was putting in.

Trina also had a top position at the modeling agency. Monica appointed her President. She ran the day to day operation of the agency. Trina approved or disapproved any new models wanting to join the agency. She also made sure that everything ran smoothly in the office. Monica paid her best friend $200,000 a year. Trina loved her job. She always had leadership qualities and now she got a chance to put them to work.

Monica and Adonis also went back to their old neighborhoods and gave jobs to old friends and people that were not doing so well. They gave them an opportunity to gain employment with them.

They also started a program as an incentive to move up in the company. The program was the brainchild of Adonis. He gave all their employees a chance to go back to college at the company's expense. The catch was that you had to major in something that would benefit Star Quality. After obtaining the degree, you had to pay back the tuition fees.

It all worked out because once you get the degree, your salary goes up, which made it easy to pay back the tuition in installments. With the pay increase, the employees were able to pay the loan back. It worked out beautifully for both employer and employee.

The Star Quality dynasty was flourishing like never before. In Monica's third year of business she doubled her previous year's income in six months. She had accounts with every major clothing company in the U.S. and a couple in France and Great Britain.

The start of their other ventures looked promising as well. The record company signed three solid acts that were very talented. One of their acts --a young rapper named FanTab-- debuted at number 5 on the billboard charts in his first week. He was selling units like hot cakes.

The movie agent branch signed five of the models from the modeling branch. They all got decent first time roles in major movies. It was a good start for a new company.

The sports branch of Star Quality signed an all-star college basketball player that was destined to go pro. They had deals on the table from the Knicks and the Celtics already. It was just a matter of which team presented the best deal.

Everything that they touched turned to platinum. They were on a roll that couldn't be stopped. As always, nature has a way of turning a perfectly clear sunny day into a hurricane.

Scandal hit the Star Quality Empire. A national tabloid magazine ran a story on Monica Nkosi, the Queen of Black modeling agencies. Her picture was posted on the cover. Inside were photos of her when she was Banana Pudding and there was talk of a video of her performing the acts. The fact that she was a stripper was old news. How damaging could that bit of information be? She thought. It didn't work when Dexter tried to ruin her with it, so why should it ruin her now? However, a video of her performing S&M on a white man devastated the company as well as Monica and Adonis' personal lives.

The video and the story that appeared in the tabloids appeared courtesy of none other than Timothy Stewart, the wealthy banker she would play the plantation game with.

Timothy sold the video and the story to the tabloids. He revealed every detail, from how he met Banana Pudding, to what she would do to him. He told them how much he paid her for her services. Timothy even let them take pictures of his back which had the scars she left on him the last time they met. He told them how she would make him call her Massa. When people saw the video, it made her look like a beast.

The heading of the article read: FORMER CALL GIRL, TURNED MODEL AGENCY EMPRESS.

No sooner than the story broke did former clients of Banana Pudding come forward with stories of sex and submission. Most of the new reports were bogus as these former clients were paid by the tabloids. Nevertheless, people were intrigued by the stories. The press was having a field day. The power of the media is great. They know that they could help or hurt a person.

The video of Monica whipping Timothy became a viral online video. It had over 1 million views in just a week. The video is what hurt the most because everyone had access to see it free on the internet.

The magnitude of the damage of the Banana Pudding stories was incredible. She was on the front page of the Gotham Post. It was their chance to tear a self-made millionaire Black woman to shreds. That's exactly what they tried to do.

Adonis was appalled at what they wrote about his wife. He knew about the stripping and he had forgiven her. Adonis then remembered their first night on their honeymoon when she hand cuffed him and made him call her Massa. That was exactly what Timothy confessed in his story. Adonis knew that Timothy was telling the truth because she played the plantation game with him. He didn't have to see the video for proof. He was deeply hurt to find out that Monica was taking part in something so uncivilized. He still loved her, but he was very hurt.

Monica and Adonis would argue every night about the stories. It got so bad at one point that Adonis didn't even want to sleep with her. He began to despise her for what she did in her past.

Monica's whole world had turned upside down in just two weeks. Everywhere she went, people recognized her as Banana Pudding. Some even taunted her and called her Massa. She couldn't escape it. She was on the cover of nearly every major magazine and newspaper. Monica received more coverage now than she did as a rap video Queen or a business mogul. She was the center of major negative press.

Things got worse when some of her accounts started to pull out of the agency. The bad thing was that they were her most lucrative accounts. The major White clothing companies did not want to be associated with a Black woman that used to whip White men who called her Massa.

The Banana Pudding scandal brought destruction to the whole Star Quality brand. She was hoping that it would all blow over before her whole dynasty came crashing down. The Star Quality Empire went from being a $100 million dollar company, to half of that in just months.

With her marriage and her business on shaky grounds, her life was now falling apart. She fell into a deep depression. Usually when she felt this depressed, she had Adonis to cheer her up, but he had not spoken to her in two weeks.

Monica started to drink her problems away. She was drunk every night after work. That only made things worse. She was decaying inside. She couldn't go on like this for much longer. It was literally killing her.

She never anticipated that something like this would happen to her, especially since she gave up stripping and sex for pay. Everything was going so well for her. Her business was flourishing and her life was great. She was feeling so sorry for herself, which was something she never did. She always had been a head strong Black woman. Now she was becoming a weak minded wreck as the days went by.

Trina knew Monica practically all of her life. She had never known her to be this depressed. Trina decided to tell her something that will uplift her spirits. "Monica, this is not you. I've watched you mope around here for the last two months and it's time to get back in gear," Trina said to her friend. "It is not the end of the world. So what they are saying all that negative stuff about you. They don't know you. They don't know what you have been through all of your life. I do. I know you are a good person. You're a survivor. You made mistakes, and *everybody* makes mistakes. The thing is learning from your mistakes."

Trina paused and then continued, "You have grown a lot as a person. Take my advice. Soon all of this news will blow over and they will find someone else to talk about. Everyone will forget all about you. Keep your head up sister. Things will get greater later. Trust me."

Monica looked at her friend with tears in her eyes. Her speech was just what Monica needed to lift her spirits. She felt a jolt of energy surging through her after hearing Trina speak.

"Thank you so much for those words of inspiration. I needed that so much." Monica hugged her friend tightly.

Eventually everything that Trina predicted happened exactly how she said it would. The scandal died down after almost six months. The press found someone else to talk about, taking all the focus off of Monica and the infamous Banana Pudding.

That eased Monica's pain and she stopped drinking. Monica and Adonis began to talk again. They attended a marriage counselor to try and salvage their marriage. The counseling was working out better than they expected. They addressed issues that helped them communicate better.

One of the issues that was hindering their communication was that Adonis was so self-righteous. He had to see that no one was perfect. People make mistakes. They even found out about one of Adonis' big mistakes that he kept a secret.

"Mr. Perfect" wasn't so perfect after all. Adonis had been having sex with his now deceased wife's best friend for years while he was married. It took a lot for him to reveal that secret. He felt so ashamed about what he had done to his wife. That was one of the reasons he felt such guilt when Tammy died.

Adonis had a belief that when a person dies, they have knowledge of everything that happened during their life. Even the secrets were revealed to them. So he believed that Tammy knew about his affair with her best friend in her afterlife.

Revealing his secret helped him understand that one person's mistake is no better than the next person's mistake. His past was no better than Monica's; understanding that concept helped him to get over the Banana Pudding chronicles once and for all.

They both assured each other that there were no more secrets to be revealed. They made a pact that everything was in the open and they could start over. The counseling brought them closer.

Monica could finally put Banana Pudding to rest. There was nothing else to tell about her past as Banana Pudding. It was all out. She thought that she had done that almost ten years ago. Apparently, it came back to haunt her. Certain things in a person's past always has a way of coming back and biting the person in the ass when she or he least expects it.

Now she was faced with the task of rebuilding the damage that was done to her company. Her marriage was saved, but her empire was drowning and she was determined to fight to save it. After all, she was a survivor! She still had some big accounts left. Star Quality Modeling Agency finished off the fiscal year doubling last year's net profit which wasn't bad. However, if it wasn't for the scandal, she would have almost had a 200% increase this year.

The other Star Quality companies didn't get hit as hard as the modeling agency did. It was probably due to the fact that Monica wasn't a direct player on those teams. She was known for being a modeling agency mogul, not for running any of the other companies that Star Quality ran.

The record company did well for its first year. The three artists that they signed went gold selling a total of 1.5 million units. Rome was going to make a return from rap retirement. He left the game with 5 million records sold. He may be able to make something happen. It had only been two years since his last album.

All in all, they went through a stormy hurricane and survived it. Even if everything fell they still had $60 million in the bank. That is more than enough to live very comfortably for six lifetimes.

How much more could you ask for? When is it enough? When does the hunger for success become greed? These are some of the questions that go through the mind of the over achiever. The answers are never the same. It is never enough to some and to others; they are content with just living a comfortable lifestyle.

For Monica and Adonis, the storm they had just survived taught them two valuable lessons. One was that a person should always expect the unexpected. And the other was that the ladder of success is always met with great adversities. Success isn't for the faint hearted.

They learned to appreciate what they had after that experience. Something or someone is always lurking in the shadows, watching and waiting for the perfect time to strike. If you're not prepared, it could be very costly, personally and financially. In the end, having each other and their family was worth more than money.

AJ was 7 years old now and his big sister, Makeda was 14. They were growing up fast. Adonis and Monica enjoyed being able to provide the best of the best for their children. Monica remembered all too well those childhood days of being neglected because of her parents' drug use.

She recalled the many days she went to bed with her little belly so hungry that it rumbled loudly and kept her awake. Monica also remembered having only having two sets of clothes to wear for a year, no Christmas gifts, no birthday gifts, and no love and no affection.

It made her the happiest woman alive to know that her children will never experience that hell. She showered them with unconditional love. She bought them whatever their hearts desired. Adonis warned her about spoiling the kids, but he understood why she was doing it.

He knew how his Queen had grown up deprived of the basic necessities of childhood. Giving her children everything worked like therapy on her soul. She felt ultimate bliss every time the children's face lit up because of something expensive that she had bought for them. Monica also realized that she had to teach them the value of hard work as well.

She felt at ease knowing that there was no chance of Makeda growing thinking about becoming a Banana Pudding like she had. Or that AJ would have to sell drugs or rob people to buy nice things.

When it was all said and done, this is what life was all about to her, providing the best for her children whom she loved more than she loved life itself. For whom she would give her last breath.

A year had passed since the Banana Pudding scandal. No one even mentioned it anymore. Life was more or less back to "normal".

The model agency never fully recovered from the storm. Monica never got back the big money accounts that she had before the scandal broke. She had to break her staff down and lease out only half of the 45th floor of the Empire State Building. It didn't really bother her much, as long as she was still in business. It gave her more time to relax and be with the family. It also gave her time to reflect on her life as a whole.

Monica was 35 years old now. She had accomplished more in the last 10 years than most people did in their entire lives. As a matter of fact, she had accomplished more than 10 people have in their entire lives. She had nothing to complain about. She was healthy and her two beautiful children and her husband were healthy.

Monica built an empire that she could pass on to her children. She had enough money to take care of her grandchildren's children. When she thought of it that way, she was satisfied with her life and her accomplishments.

Monica was still young; thirty five wasn't even middle age. She still had lots of fire in her. She was far from stopping her pursuit for more success. It was different because now she didn't have to rush for it. She felt as though she had another 35 years of fire left in her before she would retire.

She thought about if things would have turned out the same if she would not have met her King, Adonis? After a minute of thought, she said, "No." She was sure that Adonis was the inspiration that gave her the knowledge of herself. He taught her that she was special and was from royal blood. He told her that she was a Queen by nature. He didn't approach her like most men, eager to have sex with the body. He made love to her mind and then he made love to her body.

Most men will tell a woman that she was a Queen just to get her into bed. Adonis was the only man who showed and proved that she was a Queen through historical facts. That made a world of difference to a woman that was ignorant of her history.

If it wasn't for Adonis, Monica would not have even thought of stopping the stripper game. She had no intentions of being anything else. She was so naïve back then that she thought she was living the life. When she thought back on those days, she knew that she was young and foolish compared to now.

She even gave Adonis the credit for the idea of starting a Black modeling agency. She put in the work, but he gave her the thought. He was her son's father, whom she loved so much. When she really thought deeply about her success, she owed it all to her King Adonis.

I wouldn't be anything today but a stripper named Banana Pudding if it wasn't for Adonis, she thought to herself. Meeting Adonis was definitely a blessing in disguise. How would I repay this man? He is an angel sent to me. Do I pay him with my love, my utmost respect? What? Buy him a Bentley or a big platinum ring flooded with ice, an expensive yacht? Throw him the biggest party in honor of his name? None of these things would amount to how much reverence I have for this man.

She knew Adonis too well. He didn't like material things that much. He was content with the basics. He wouldn't really accept a Bentley or a yacht, or any of those material things. She knew what Adonis would appreciate most of all. More than anything, he would love something simple; a walk in the park or a walk along the beach watching the sun set, a greeting card that read I LOVE YOU MORE, candlelight dinner with just the two of them.

That's what she loved about this man, a man with so much knowledge, a man so preciously special, a man so rare. He valued the simple things that life had to offer. He would appreciate the thought that his Queen loved him enough to *want* to make him feel special. That was all he needed. She could gladly give that to him from the core of her being.

After an hour of meditating in her office on the 45th floor, she put on her full length mink coat and paged her driver to pull the limo out. She took the elevator downstairs and got into the Lincoln Town car limousine that was waiting for her.

As she sat in the plush leather seats of luxury and turned on the TV, she said, "Not bad at all for a poor Black girl from Bedford-Stuyvesant, Brooklyn with no education...Formerly known as Banana Pudding. Not bad at all, if I do say so myself."

CHAPTER 19

Back in Bedford-Stuyvesant, Brooklyn at the 79th precinct, Detectives Brown and Santiago were still on the trail of Cagney. They still had no real leads to her true identity or her whereabouts. Brown vowed to catch her if it was the last thing he did in his career.

Brown was about to retire in two years. He didn't have much time left before his career as a homicide detective was over. His partner, Santiago, had quite a few years left before his retirement, so he could take up the pursuit of Cagney after Brown retired. Santiago had only been on the force as a detective for three years. He had learned a great deal from his veteran partner, Brown.

Brown had an outstanding reputation as a homicide detective. He had over a thousand arrests under his belt and 800 of those arrests resulted in a conviction. When he caught his suspect, he made sure that he had the right man. Out of all his arrests, 200 of them were women and 115 of those were acquitted at trial. He had a gut instinct that told him every night that there was a blood-thirsty female killer out there. She was not going to stop until he put an end to her ravenous appetite for murder. Brown never wanted to arrest a murder suspect this much in his entire career. He became obsessed with arresting Cagney.

Cagney was smart. At every turn, she was out smarting them. She was quick and resourceful. That's what Brown liked about her. It was almost like he was romantically attracted to the idea that she was so cunning. He wanted to finally catch her so that he could meet her face to face and look in her eyes while talking to her. Sometimes Brown got an erection thinking about catching Cagney.

Nowadays, Brown's erections were stimulated by his new lover, Detective Lisa Harris from the 81st precinct. They had made it a regularity of seeing each other after that first meeting when Brown went to visit her. Being homicide detectives was fuel in their romantic fireplace.

They couldn't get enough of each other. Detective Harris' sexual appetite was almost animalistic. Brown had to adapt to her hunger. After a few sexual sessions with her, he began to crave her just as much. They were a match made in Police heaven.

One day while Brown and Santiago were delivering a suspect to Rikers Island, they overheard two young thugs in training. They were in the bull pen talking loudly to one another about Cagney. Brown couldn't help but listen to the youths talking about Cagney.

"Yo son, that bitch is official. I'm telling you son. One time I heard the bitch robbed this nigga for $100,000 and 3 keys. She made the nigga think she wasn't going to kill him. When he reached for his gun, she gave it to him. Blong! Blong! Blong! Right in the chest." He emphasized the sound Blong.

Then the other youth gave his exaggerated version of the tale. "And yo, that bitch is an expert marksman. She don't miss son. I heard one time the bitch had to kill some nigga but when she went to get him, he was holding his daughter. The bitch doesn't kill kids. From a block away, she aimed and shot duke tight between the eyes without touching the little girl."

"Get the fuck out of here son! You just made that shit up. You free styling right now."

"That's my word son. Scooter told me. He was right there when it happened."

"What does she look like then?"

"She was light skinned. Bad... With a fat ass."

"Now I know you lying because don't nobody know what Cagney looks like. She always wears a disguise."

The other youths started laughing.

Brown and Santiago couldn't help but let out a little laugh themselves. They left their suspect on Rikers. Brown was deep in thought. Santiago noticed that his partner was thinking about something.

"Hey Brown, what's on your mind?"

Brown turned to his younger partner and looked at him with his infamous look of seriousness on his face and said, "THE LEGEND OF CAGNEY."

Monica and Adonis were home alone. AJ and Makeda were at Rome's house with Tavon for the weekend. The candles were burning so long that they were melting down into a small puddle of wax.

The dinner that they had just devoured was Adonis' favorite dish; smoked salmon with asparagus and tofu. Monica was preparing the meal all day. She wanted it to be perfect. They were drinking a chilled bottle of Port vintage wine and relaxing on the couch.

The atmosphere was very subtle and peaceful. Just for two days they had no business, no kids, and no interruptions. It was just the two of them together.

They cherished the little time they had alone as a couple. With their busy schedules, this was a luxury for them. Every second in time was like a treat. They knew that they had to make the most of this precious weekend. There was no telling when they may get to do this again.

The TV was off and all of the lights were dim. Adonis got up to put a CD on. It was a mixed CD of all the best songs of the 80's and 90's. Boys to Men's classic 1991 hit song; 'TO THE END OF THE ROAD' was the first song.

"Boo, I love this song. Oh honey, this song brings back so many memories," Monica said.

"I was in NYU when this song came out. College was so fun back then. It seems like it was all over too fast."

"I never had a chance to go to college. I wish I would've gone to college when I was younger. I missed out on a lot," said Monica.

"It's never too late to go back to school. I remember this 50 year old woman was in my Human Resource Management class."

"You know what? I think that's what I'm going to do. You always give me good advice. I don't know what I would be or where I'd be if I had not met my king." Monica kissed Adonis softly on the lips.

"I believe that nothing happens by coincidence or chance. I believe that everything that has happened happens for a reason. It was in our destiny to cross paths and fulfill our legacy. You filled that empty void that I had when Tammy died. I know somewhere in the afterlife, Tammy is happy that I'm with someone like you. You are a very unique woman."

"Coming from you, that is a compliment. I have never met a man as fascinating as you my King."

They kissed after the serenade to each other's special qualities.

Another song came over the stereo that was popular in 1992---TLC's 'BABY, BABY, BABY'.

"Oh Adonis, this used to be my favorite song back in the days. I love TLC. That is so sad that Left Eye died at such a young age. She was so talented. The world will miss her." She paused to give a moment of silence. She then sang, "Baby, baby, baby. I got so much love for you."

She sang the words to Adonis making him blush like a teen. She grabbed his hands and pulled him off the couch. She began to slowly, seductively dance with him. Whenever she danced like this, it reminded her of her strip club days as Banana Pudding. She didn't care because dancing was something that she enjoyed, even before she became Banana Pudding.

They danced and sang the songs for hours. They were having so much fun that they lost all sense of time. It had been some time since they had a chance to unwind like this. After the CD's were finished, they sat down on the couch.

"That was fun," Monica said with exhaustion. "We should do that more often to release tension."

"You wore me out honey. You can dance all night."

Whenever Adonis thought about Monica dancing, it reminded him of Banana Pudding. It brought up ill feelings of the time when she was Banana Pudding. He didn't take them any further than a feeling. He learned to let them go. He learned to let them just pass. He learned not to harp on his thoughts. Adonis knew that letting go of negative thoughts helped their relationship.

Monica knew what he was thinking whenever dancing was mentioned. She knew him all too well, possibly better than he knew himself.

"I know what you're thinking honey and it's all right. We can be open about anything. There is nothing to hide anymore." She paused to look into his eyes. "Yes, I can dance longer than the average person because I use to be a stripper called Banana Pudding. But because of you, I learned that I can be much more than that. Because of you, I learned that I'm a Queen and you're my King."

Adonis knew that his Queen was being sincere and he admired her for that.

"Can I ask you a question?" Adonis asked.

"Sure, you can ask me anything."

"Why did they call you Banana Pudding? I wanted to ask you that for the longest."

She put her arms around his neck and kissed him passionately. In a low, sexy tone she spoke into his ear, "Because my skin is yellow like a banana." She paused to kiss him slowly and softly. "And my pussy is creamy like pudding. And it is all yours my King." She kissed him again, only longer this time.

"That makes sense when you put it that way."

Monica looked Adonis in his eyes. She chose her next words carefully. She spoke with the utmost of sincerity.

"I want to thank you, Adonis."

"Thank me for what?" Adonis asked.

"For being so understanding, for helping me find myself and showing me who I really am. Before I met you, I was lost. I was living life like a savage in the pursuit of happiness. I thought I was happy but in reality I wasn't...Until I met you. You bring me joy. You were like the sun in my world that was filled with darkness. For this, I am eternally grateful to you."

The reverence in her voice was so sincere that it almost brought Adonis to tears. He replied with their old saying. "Don't mention it," Adonis said with a smile.

Adonis picked his Queen up, cradled her in his arms and carried her to their bedroom. Then they made sweet love until the sun rose in the East the next day.

THE END

CHECK OUT THE SPIN OFF FROM BANANA PUDDING!

THE LEGEND OF CAGNEY...

The ruthless female assassin that was first introduced in Banana Pudding, Cagney, will leave you in suspense in her own fast-paced murder mystery. Cagney is the master of deception and disguise. That's why she is a legend.

Here is a sneak peek into the wild world of the most dangerous Black woman assassin. If you like tales of murder and mystery with an intellectual twist, you are going to love THE LEGEND OF CAGNEY!!!

ANOTHER HOT NOVEL BY

ALAH ADAMS

CHAPTER 1

The wind was blowing so hard that it howled like an injured wolf in a forest. It would have been just cold, but the wind brought the chill factor to freezing. There wasn't any snow on the ground as of yet; however New York City felt like Alaska.

It was November, one week from Thanksgiving. You could already feel the Holiday spirit in the atmosphere. Women were already packing the local supermarkets getting all of the trimmings for the historic day of *giving*. So it is said to be.

Other than a few Holiday shoppers going into stores, the streets of West Harlem were fairly empty. There was one mysterious-looking woman walking up Amsterdam Avenue.

One glance at the fairly tall woman and you would think that she was wearing some type of disguise. She wore a full length black leather trench coat. She had on a blond wig that was covered with a Fendi scarf tied under her chin. She wore big Chanel sunglasses that hid her facial expression. It was hard to figure out how this woman looked.

The reason it seemed she was wearing a disguise was because she was. The mysterious woman was known as Cagney to her clients. She had good reasons to hide her true identity. Cagney was the most sought after assassin in New York City. The only reason she lasted this long was because no one knew what she looked like, except for her little sister, Tamika.

There were questions about if she really existed. Was this infamous female hit woman real or was she just one of the 6 million stories told in the naked city? That's what made Cagney a legend.

In the underworld of big time crime, she was very real. She was very good at what she did. Cagney was the best assassin that money could buy.

Ten years ago, Cagney had a partner named Lacey. Together they were known as Cagney and Lacey, named after the hit TV series in the 80's. Lacey got killed at a botched hit requested by a local drug dealer named Big Walt. They were amateurs back then. They made a lot of mistakes on that job, mistakes that Lacey paid for with her life.

Cagney missed her partner and best friend, Lacey. They had grown up together in the Flatbush section of Brooklyn. They were first introduced into a life of crime by two drug dealers named Carlos and Ray-Ray. They moonlighted as stick up kids.

Carlos and Ray-Ray would have Cagney and Lacey date other big time drug dealers and then set them up for the kill. They were good at setting up dealers because they were highly attractive. Women have been one of many drug dealers weakness, and ultimately, the cause of their demise.

Their criminal activities became an obsession. They began to carry guns daily. They quickly became infatuated with guns. They learned everything there was to learn about them, like how to clean them and how to aim properly. They knew all the different types of guns just by looking at them. They quickly became gun specialists.

Carlos and Ray-Ray had created monsters that were like two vicious pit bulls. You know what happens when you don't treat pit bulls right? They snap and turn on you.

Cagney and Lacey knew that Carlos and Ray-Ray were using them. They grew tiresome of helping them rob balers for thousands and only getting a couple of hundred dollars for their labor. That labor often required them to sleep with their victims to get their trust. Their so-called boyfriends condoned it.

"Do whatever you have to do to soften these lames up. Fuck them, suck their dicks, do whatever it takes," Carlos said.

They didn't care about Cagney and Lacey at all. They had new cars, expensive jewelry and nice clothes. They would ride around with other females right in Cagney and Lacey's face. They would only come around to get them when they wanted the duo to set up dealers, but the girls were tired of being played like fools. Enough was enough.

They were all at Carlos's house counting money from a big hit. They robbed a heroin dealer for $200,000 in cash. That was the most money they took at one time. Carlos was so loose and carefree around the girls that he opened the safe in front of them. The safe had so much money in it that there was no room left for anymore. Cagney's eyes lit up. Now is the time, she thought.

Cagney gave Lacey the signal and they both pulled out twin 357 magnum revolvers. Carlos turned around and smiled at the sight of the two females with their guns drawn.

His partner, Ray-Ray was in the bathroom. When he came out, Lacey pointed her gun at him.

"Get over there with Carlos and sit your ass down," Lacey said to him in a serious tone.

"What's going on?" Ray-Ray asked

"You know that the fuck it is!" Cagney answered.

"Come on baby," Carlos said smoothly. "If its money you want all you had to do was ask."

As he spoke, he slowly reached for his gun. Ray-Ray was also reaching for his weapon. The two men were foolish for reaching for their guns. They didn't think that their two protégés were capable of shooting them. Why they thought that was beyond Cagney and Lacey.

The girls saw them inching for their guns. Cagney knew they had to murder Carlos and Ray-Ray. Robbing them for this much money and leaving them living was suicide on their part.

Cagney and Lacey looked at each other and nodded their heads. Without a word, they both dumped rounds into Carlos and Ray-Ray. Cagney unloaded hers into Carlos, her so-called man. And Lacey gave it to her so-called man, Ray-Ray. The two men were laid out in a pool of their own blood.

Cagney filled up two small suitcases with money. Lacey grabbed the keys to Carlos's Lexus. They ran out of the apartment and drove into the night.

Neither one saw the old woman that was looking out of the window. When the detectives came to the scene, she told them what she saw. The only thing that she could make out was that the two Black women wore wigs. That is how Detectives Brown and Santiago got involved in the case.

Cagney poured gas inside and outside of the Lexus and set it on fire. When Brown and Santiago began their investigation, all they had was a torched Lexus and an old woman's statement, which summed up to zero.

There was $500,000 in cash in that safe. Cagney and Lacey went on a spending spree. Cagney bought her little sister a new Mercedes CLK and a nice apartment. Lacey spent all of her money on herself. She didn't have any brothers and sisters and no family that she cared for.

Cagney and Lacey spent all of the money in 6 months. When the money was all gone, that's when they came up with the idea to go into business as hit women. They figured since they loved guns and violence, they may as well get paid for it.

When they first started, business was slow. In fact there was no business at all. No one took them seriously. They decided to go back to robbing drug dealers again.

Soon that became dangerous. They weren't killing their victims. The word spread about Cagney and Lacey robbing everything moving. They had so many drug dealers put contracts on them that they had to wear disguises every day.

They became so infamous for sticking up drug dealers that people began to give them a name. That's how things go in the hood. Someone will always come up with a name for something. Someone started calling them Cagney and Lacey. Before you know it, the whole NYC was talking about Cagney and Lacey.

There were ten different drug dealers that wanted Cagney and Lacey's head on a platter. The dealers were determined to kill them. So Cagney and Lacey did what they felt had to be done for their survival. They started killing all of their victims one by one. They went back and murdered all the dealers they had previously robbed.

That's when the contracts for hits started rolling in. The last contract that Cagney and Lacey did as a team was 10 years ago on Gates Ave. That was when Lacey got killed. Cagney was minutes from being arrested by Detective Brown.

Cagney was shot in the chest three times that day. Luckily, she had on a vest. The impact from the slugs still knocked her unconscious. When the police arrived on the scene, they thought she was an innocent bystander that got caught in the crossfire. They took her to the hospital in an ambulance.

While she was in the hospital, Detective Brown put two and two together and figured out that she wasn't an innocent bystander. Brown had the gut feeling that she was Cagney and he was right.

Brown called Kings County Hospital to confirm that he was feeling. When the nurse told him that she was wearing a wig, Brown knew he finally had her.

However, it was not going to be easy for Brown. Cagney overheard the conversation that the nurse was having with Brown. She was in pain, but she knew she had to get out of there. She got of the bed, got dressed and strolled out of the hospital. She caught a cab. Just as she was leaving the hospital, Brown and Santiago were pulling in. They missed her by seconds.

That was the closest that Brown came to catching Cagney. She knew all about Brown's devoted pursuit of her. Till this day, Brown couldn't figure out how she was able to elude them for so long. She was always seven steps ahead of them. How she was able to do it was a mystery to Brown. Soon the saga of the legendary Cagney will unfold.

I have a nice surprise for Brown, Cagney thought to herself.

Cagney finally reached her destination. She was looking for 657 Amsterdam Ave. Apt. 27A. She was always nervous about meeting a new customer. It could be a set up with the police.

Cagney had ways of knowing when her customers were legit. She was a professional, and any modern day professional knows how use technology to their advantage. Cagney had more gadgets than Inspector Gadget himself.

She pressed the intercom button for Apt 27A. A man with a thick Latin accent answered.

"Is that you, Cagney?" the voice asked.

"Yeah."

The door buzzed, signaling for her to enter. She went to the second floor and saw 27A on a door. She pulled out her .45 Caliber with a silencer and tapped the door.

"The door is open sweetheart."

She opened the door and entered with her gun out. There were three men in the living room sitting on a couch. There was loud Spanish music coming from the TV. The men made a sudden reaching movement when they saw Cagney with her gun out.

"I wouldn't do that if I were you," Cagney warned them. "Be real easy."

She went to each of the men and disarmed them. Then she took out a device from her pocket the size of a beeper. She ran it across each man's chest and waist. It

231

was a bug detector. If there was any listening device in the apartment, the detector would go off.

"OK gentlemen. Everything is all good. Let's get down to business."

"I like your style. Very umm…How you say." His thick accent made him hard to understand. "Yes, very professional. My name is Green Eyes. It is nice to finally meet you, Cagney."

"The pleasure is all mines. Now enough of the small talk," Cagney replied in a serious tone.

There was a folder on the table. Green Eyes grabbed it and handed it to Cagney. In it were 10 photos of 10 different men. She studied the photos carefully. It was hard for her to focus with the lights so dim and the dark glasses she wore. She couldn't risk taking them off and showing her true identity, however.

"Those ten guys run a rival company. You do understand that we like to refer to our drug business as companies." Cagney nodded, wanting to be spared the rhetoric. "They come from my country in Santa Domingo. They have come to New York and taken over all of Washington Heights. They have cut a hole so deep into my pockets that I'm barely eating. They call themselves the Moreno Cartel because they are all dark skinned. They will be in New York for Thanksgiving at this address. I want them all dead. I'm willing to pay you $50,000 a head. That's $500,000 all together."

Cagney thought about the challenge ahead of her. This would be the biggest contract of her career.

"I'll accept the job, but I want half the money up front today."

"How do I know that you won't take the money and disappear? You are a very hard woman to find."

Cagney sensed something sneaky in his statement. She was a good judge of character. Her senses were tingling.

"Listen, Green Eyes. I don't play any games. The person that referred you to me can verify that. Matter fact, I don't have time for this." She made a motion for the door.

"Please wait!" Green Eyes pleaded. "I'll give you $150,000 today and I'll give you the rest after you get the job done, deal?"

She had to think about that for a minute. Usually she would have turned him down immediately, but she needed the money.

$150,000 is enough money to hold me down, she thought.

"OK Green Eyes, I'll take the $150,000 for now. But if you don't pay me the rest of my money, I'll take pleasure in killing you for free."

"I understand. I like a woman that knows how to take charge."

Cagney knew that his comment was meant to flatter her. It would have worked with the average female, but Cagney was not the average woman.

Green Eyes handed her a briefcase with $150,000 in it. "It is my pleasure to do business with you Cagney." Green opened the door for her. He stuck his hand out for a handshake.

She had her gun in one hand and the briefcase in the other, so she couldn't shake the Green's hand, she left him hanging.

Order Form!

Make a Pre-order of 'THE LEGEND OF CAGNEY'

Please Print:

Title #1 _____

Title #2 _____

Name _____

Address_____

City _____**State**_____

Zip_____

Phone (   )_____

___copies of book @ $14.95each$_____
Postage and handling @ $4.00per book$_____
Total amount enclosed$_____
Make checks payable to:
Gully Multi-Media
P.O. Box 3602
Laurel, MD 20707
ALL INMATES RECEIVE A 20% DISCOUNT! $11.95
Legend of Cagney will be shipped to you on or before
December 2010!
ORDER ONLINE AT GULLYMULTIMEDIA.COM **TO WIN
GIFTS AND GET DISCOUNTS ON BOOKS, MUSIC AND
VIDEOS!!**

Banana Pudding   *By Alah Adams*

ABOUT THE AUTHOUR

Alah Adams is not only an author; he is also a songwriter, music producer, and a rap artist. While Alah was incarcerated for selling narcotics, he wrote seven novels. The first of the seven novels to be released is **Banana Pudding,** which has a soundtrack single that was written and produced by Alah Adams. The other six novels will be released in three to six month intervals. **The Legend of Cagney** will be the next novel, followed by **Project Horizon (with soundtrack), King Poppa (with soundtrack), Vengeance of Cagney (book 2), Ice Cream, and Cagney's Last Stand (book 3).**

Alah Adams is a proud father of four, and a longtime resident of Long Island, New York

LOG ONTO WWW.GULLYMULTIMEDIA.COM TO HEAR THE NEW MUSIC FROM THE AUTHOR, INCLUDING VIDEOS AND TO WIN PRIZES AND MORE!!!